"Damn If You Don't Tie Me In Knots," Sean Growled.

"I'm trying to untie you," Julia said.

"Maybe that's what this is."

"This?"

He pressed a fist to his chest. "The feeling of knots loosening." He turned suddenly and looked at her, hard, then leaned over.

Adrenaline, desire, something instinctive made her part her lips. For one excruciating moment, she wanted him to confess that what she'd been feeling since the first morning in her office was mutual, that this heady combination of desire and confusion was reciprocal.

He put his finger on her bottom lip and rubbed slowly back and forth. Desire spiraled in every direction as heat beaded her breastbone with perspiration.

Sean touched her hair, then pulled back. "I should be arrested for what I'm thinking...."

Dear Reader:

News flash!

The Branigans Are Back!

All of you who have written over the years to say how much you love Leslie Davis Guccione's BRANIGAN BROTHERS will be thrilled and pleased that this rambunctious family is back with *Branigan's Break*.

More Fun from Lass Small!

We start the New Year with a fun-filled *Man of the Month* from one of your favorite writers. Don't miss *A Nuisance*, which is what our man makes of himself this month!

The Return of Diana Mars!

So many readers have wondered, "Where is Diana Mars?" This popular author took a break from writing, but we're excited that she's now writing for Silhouette Desire with *Peril in Paradise*.

Christmas in January!

For those of you who can't get enough of the holidays, please don't let Suzannah Davis's charming *A Christmas Cowboy* get away.

Mystery and Danger...

In Modean Moon's *Interrupted Honeymoon*.

Baby, Baby...

In Shawna Delacorte's *Miracle Baby*.

So start the New Year right with Silhouette Desire!

With all best wishes for a great 1995,

Lucia Macro
Senior Editor

Please address questions and book requests to:
Silhouette Reader Service
U.S.: 3010 Walden Ave., P.O. Box 1325, Buffalo, NY 14269
Canadian: P.O. Box 609, Fort Erie, Ont. L2A 5X3

LESLIE DAVIS GUCCIONE
BRANIGAN'S BREAK

SILHOUETTE *Desire*®

Published by Silhouette Books

America's Publisher of Contemporary Romance

For Alfie and Ellen

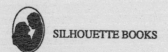

SILHOUETTE BOOKS

ISBN 0-373-05902-7

BRANIGAN'S BREAK

LESLIE DAVIS GUCCIONE

now writes from Pittsburgh, Pennsylvania. After twenty years in rural Duxbury, Massachusetts, she and her family are enjoying city life. In addition to writing romances, Leslie is the award-winning author of books for middle grade and young adult readers.

BRANIGAN FAMILY TREE

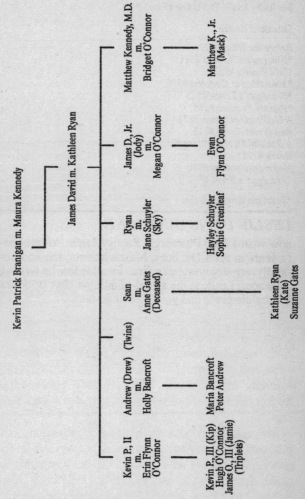

Kevin Patrick Branigan m. Maura Kennedy

James David m. Kathleen Ryan

Kevin P., II
m.
Erin Flynn
O'Connor

Andrew (Drew) (Twins)
m.
Holly Bancroft

Sean
m.
Anne Gates
(Deceased)

Ryan
m.
Jane Schuyler
(Sky)

James D., Jr.
(Jody)
m.
Megan O'Connor

Matthew Kennedy, M.D.
m.
Bridget O'Connor

Kevin P., III (Kip)
Hugh O'Connor
James O., III (Jamie)
(Triplets)

Maria Bancroft
Peter Andrew

Kathleen Ryan
(Kate)
Suzanne Gates

Hayley Schuyler
Sophie Greenleaf

Evan
Flynn O'Connor

Matthew K., Jr.
(Mack)

One

Millbrook Middle School adjustment counselor Julia Hollins hurried from the faculty lounge toward her office in the administrative department as the second-period bell rang. She negotiated the school corridors, dodging sixth, seventh and eighth graders, the occasional adult, and the hallway sculpture display on loan from the high school art department. Her secretary had paged her because Sean Branigan had arrived, apparently in hopes of seeing his daughter's history teacher, Alfie Forbes. However, the elusive man hadn't made an appointment and Alfie was on a field trip.

Her mind had been on her own children, not the students. Brett needed another reference book for his economics course at Harvard. Nick, struggling to make friends as a new junior at Millbrook High School, had been teased for spending the last two soccer games on the bench. Now he insisted that owning his own car would help immensely. So would winning the lottery, she'd pointed out. So would less lavish, self-indulgent living on the part of her ex-husband, though she didn't voice that in front of the boys.

For the five years she'd been divorced, little or no self-indulgence on her part had kept the small family comfortable. When the opening for Millbrook Middle School adjustment counselor had appeared in the *Boston Globe,* she'd jumped at the chance to relocate from Boston's tonier, expensive suburbs. The small, picturesque town deep in Plymouth County had excellent public schools and was far enough off the beaten path to still have housing she could afford. She accepted the position on her thirty-ninth birthday, convinced by her eldest child, Brett, who was tasting college dormitory life in Cambridge, that it was the right thing to do, as much for his younger brother as for herself. Nick had not been so easy to convince.

The Millbrook schools complex sprawled in three campus-style buildings, separated by their playing fields and playgrounds on rolling acres at the edge of the town limits. Julia's office and the children she cared for were in the middle.

She pushed aside thoughts of her sons and tried to recall what scant information Alfie Forbes had given her on eighth grader Kate Branigan, the feisty redhead she'd had in detention all week. The teenager's father was busy, hard to reach, had Alfie said, often out of town? Alfie's complaints were numerous and painfully familiar to Julia. As a single mother she often answered for her own children's absentee father. Unfortunately, the history teacher with concerns about her recalcitrant student was also out of town—in Plymouth on a field trip—which left Julia to conduct the impromptu conference for which she was unprepared.

Julia Hollins hated to appear unknowledgeable. She was new to the school system, just five weeks into her job, and Kate was not a priority. Although the student was in no serious trouble, Alfie had used Julia as a sounding board out of concern because the teenager was floundering in her history class, as well as math, and there had been a detention or two already.

As Julia walked the length of the building, she mentally pulled together scraps of Alfie's conversations and the meager information the teacher had given her. She should have made time for the conference Alfie had requested with her. She should have put together a file with more in it than the child's name and her detention slips.

What she remembered most clearly was the teacher's concern about Kate's living arrangements and the inability to get "the elusive Sean Branigan," as Alfie called him, to sit down for a conference. Julia berated herself as she reached the administrative wing. What had Alfie mentioned? This teenager lived part-time with her elusive father? Alfie thought the eighth grader's life lacked structure.

Boundaries within a loving environment were essential ingredients to any child's well-being. Julia intended to point that out as diplomatically as possible. The rest of the conference she'd have to play by ear, based on the man himself and what he was expecting.

Julia paused outside her office long enough to adjust the scarf around her neck, tuck a wisp of hair behind her ear and take a deep breath. She forced a

smile, reminded herself of the importance of eye contact and opened her office door. What she found
across the room stopped her in her tracks.

The man in her office was seated in the chair in
front of her window, backlighted by the clear Sep-
tember sky and the morning sun that played in the
sugar maple behind him. The collar of his tartan flan-
nel shirt peaked from beneath a well-worn cable-knit
sweater, a frayed cuff skimmed his knuckle just above
a wedding band. Had Alfie mentioned a remarriage,
a stepmother?

His legs were stretched out in front of him, chino
covered and capped in work boots. They were crossed
at the ankle, left boot over right. His head was cocked
to one side, which had forced a lock of his thick dark
hair over his eyebrow. His expression was unread-
able.

Sean Branigan was sound asleep.

Nearly twenty years as a fire fighter and emergency
medical technician, combined with the erratic schedule demanded by the family cranberry business, had
taught Sean to sleep briefly, soundly and to awake
fully alert.

As he dozed, pressure on his shoulder registered first
in his unconscious as warmth. By the time his brain
interpreted it as the touch of a hand, Sean was awake.
He opened his eyes. The pale blur sharpened and registered as the drape of a paisley scarf. Breasts swayed
under shifting scarlet silk. He blinked and straightened in the chair. Arousal teased him briefly. He
flushed.

"Mr. Branigan?"

He stood, head and shoulders above the woman in front of him. She resembled the teenagers in the photograph on her desk, one he'd stared at in an effort to stay awake as he'd waited for her. Now he looked into the crown of her head: coffee-colored hair piled into some sort of knot that seemed to defy gravity. She touched her hair, then the knot of her scarf. He was fully alert.

Confusion flickered as she knit her brows. Her expression was full of concern, then composure. Her brown eyes were wide, framed in dark, straight lashes. She seemed a bit flushed herself.

"Mr. Branigan?" she repeated.

"Yes." He yawned. "Dr. Holland?" As the last vestiges of sleep evaporated, his irritation returned.

She offered her hand. "Hollins."

He shook it and straightened. "I'm sorry I dozed off while I was waiting for you. Frost warnings. I was monitoring our bogs most of the night."

"Cranberries. I understand you're part of the Branigan Company. I'm new to Millbrook, but I know this is cranberry country. You must be getting ready for the harvest."

"Yes, we are."

"Would you like some coffee or tea?"

"No, thank you. I don't have much time and I'd like to get to the point. I was expecting to see Mrs. Forbes. She's called me a few times, and I know she wants to iron out some of Kate's troubles with history."

"The office told you she was on a field trip, I hope."

"Yes. They suggested I see you. Kate doesn't need a psychologist."

"I'm the adjustment counselor."

"It's a politically correct term for school psychologist, isn't it?"

"Does that bother you?"

His laugh was sardonic. "Proof enough."

"That it bothers you?"

"That you're a psychologist. You people always answer questions with questions."

"Do we?" When he arched his eyebrow in reply, she laughed. "I'm sorry, I couldn't resist."

Something in his chest stirred at her effort and her deep brown gaze. *Evaluation.* He straightened his shoulders.

"I've replaced Ellen Reynolds. She retired last June." She motioned for him to sit back down, as she settled into the chair at her desk. "Part of my job is to be aware of detentions and what they're for, as well as to check up on youngsters who might be struggling academically. Alfie is fond of Kate and concerned that she's having a rough time so early in the school year."

She seemed expectant, hopeful no doubt, that he might spill his guts without too much effort on her part. He wondered how much time Kate had spent in here without telling him.

Kate, the imp who led the pack of Branigan cousins, was a constant source of joy and frustration, closer to any one of her five aunts than she was to him. Puberty had shaved off the edges of her tomboyish vitality and left glimpses of the young woman she would become. In the meantime, however, he was left with a budding teenager who slammed her door one minute and threw her arms around his neck the next. It was exhausting.

"She had a tough time with the European explorers and getting their settlements straight," Sean finally replied.

"Alfie's concerned about the misplaced homework papers, books left at different locations, a myriad of excuses for late or nonexistent work. I've had a similar report from her math teacher." She settled behind her desk, under a framed poster of Plimoth Plantation. No doubt a history lover. He glanced around for a bust of Freud.

Her scarf was now perfectly arranged over her shoulder. Julia Hollins's extraordinary eyes were balanced by lips that shone with a fresh application of gloss, close to the color of her scarf. The effect was pleasant. She was very pretty. She was also very confidant, the perfect balance of concern and professional distance. The good ones always were.

She was clearly in her element. The room was as neat as she was, orderly, deceivingly cheerful. No busts of Freud, but posters and prints in appropriate places: an antidrug design over the double set of file cabinets, near the window one from the Monet exhibit at the Boston Museum of Fine Arts. The chairs were comfortable. An ambience designed to inspire confidence, he presumed, in parents and students.

Forty-two years old and he still remembered this room. Orphaned at sixteen, it was the same office he and his five brothers had been yanked into under the well-intentioned efforts of the now-retired Ellen Reynolds and the Massachusetts Department of Social Services.

He'd come over from the high school, herded with the rest of the Branigan brothers from all three school buildings by the school and state authorities for monthly therapy sessions with their guardian Peter Bancroft.

Being excused from class—a forced march across the campus for the rest of his high school career—had only deepened Sean's sense of alienation. His classmate Annie Gates had been the single feminine bright spot in his life. In an attempt to escape the chaos, he'd married her as soon as he'd graduated and settled on fire fighting as an auxiliary career to the family business.

Well after he was out of the school system, he still reassured his youngest brothers that these people wouldn't separate them. How many times had all the brothers listened to the assurances that the school authorities only had the Branigans' best interest at heart?

"We all have Kate's best interest at heart, Mr. Branigan."

He shook his head. He should never have come here with so little sleep and even less patience for snoopy psychologists.

Dr. Hollins's gaze darkened as she tried to capture his attention. "We're concerned about her. I'm sorry Alfie isn't here to talk with you herself, but it might be beneficial to all of us if you started with me, anyway."

"Kate doesn't need analysis."

"Of course she doesn't. She is, however, struggling in a few areas and I think maybe some of the episodes indicate that."

"Episodes? You're referring to the smoking in the locker room. It was a dare that she regrets. No one in her family smokes."

"The trash can caught fire. It set off the emergency sprinkler system."

"I know. She was trying to destroy the evidence. Kate more than most is aware of the dangers of fire. It won't happen again."

"I don't think any of us is worried about Kate starting fires. It's her self-esteem, her sense of achievement that's important. You do know that Kate has detention this week for skipping the assembly last Friday. I've allowed her to serve it here during lunch and study hall so she doesn't miss soccer."

"She hasn't mentioned it." Across the desk he could see that the signature on the parental detention notice read "Holly Bancroft Branigan." No doubt there was a conspiracy to keep the information from him. He kept that revelation to himself.

"We're flexible in these things. I know how important the soccer team is to her. While she's here, I'd like to review her study skills. She might like a study group if she thinks it would help with her assignments. Millbrook has a wonderful peer tutoring program. She could easily be matched with a strong math and history student, for example, a junior or senior from the high school who'd meet with her once or twice a week. Often kids like Kate are much more likely to ask questions and accept help from a peer then they are from a teacher."

"Kids like Kate?"

"Who need a boost. We're here for the students, Mr. Branigan."

Her gaze never left him. He felt it on his cheek as if she'd put her fingers there, as if she could read every defensive thought in his head. He glanced at the photograph again, half inclined to turn the tables and ask about her own children, irrelevant as it was.

She cleared her throat. "I understand that Kate lives with you part-time."

"We've worked out what's best for Kate and her sister. It has to be that way with my schedule. Shifts at the firehouse after cranberry season make some weeks impossible. I do some regional work, travel on behalf of Millbrook's Emergency Medical System as well as the cranberry business. The girls are with me when it's possible."

"But without a set pattern?"

He moved to the edge of his chair. "There's plenty of pattern. It just changes from time to time."

Through the window the breeze drove maple leaves into a frenzied dance as they drifted to the ground. Bare soon, cold soon. The fatigue he always fought this time of year nearly smothered him.

"Dr. Hollins, an older student to tutor her is fine with me, but I don't want Millbrook's adjustment counselor—you or anyone else—poking and pestering my daughter."

His reluctance came from an adolescence full of explaining, a lifetime of analysis and misplaced sympathy by well-meaning people. His ribs ached. He'd been through this so many times he already anticipated the concern and pity he knew would sweep into her voice and shade her eyes. He hated it, had always hated it. Guilt, anger, vestiges of grief had left permanent bruises. Branigans against the world: Dr. Reynolds had said it all those years before. There was still an element of truth to it.

Sean stood. "I blame myself for coming over here without an appointment, but I thought I was just going to see Kate's teacher. Both my daughters have rules and boundaries, Dr. Hollins. Their home life may not be as conventional as the school would like, but it's structured, nurturing and as full of love as you can find."

Julia was already on her feet. Confusion, concern darkened her complexion. "Don't misunderstand me. I think joint custody can work beautifully under the right circumstances. It's just important for someone Kate's age to have the same set of rules and boundaries from both parents."

"Both parents?" His heart jumped at her ignorance.

Julia took a deep breath to calm her racing pulse. *Elusive* didn't begin to describe the complexities of the man in front of her. He turned to the window and shut her out as if he'd slammed a door between them.

He spoke to the window. "You people always want what's best for your students. I understand that, but it doesn't mean we—they—aren't entitled to their privacy."

Julia put her hand on his arm but pulled back as her fingers trembled against the wool of his sweater. "Mr. Branigan, I've offended you. I'm sorry."

He closed his eyes and shook his head. "You didn't offend me. I just presumed you knew Kate's situation. It's all in the school files. Believe me, Dr. Reynolds had one an inch thick on Kate. No doubt the elementary school has the same on Suzanne."

She followed his gaze out the window. A gym class was doing calisthenics. "I would have studied Kate's records if I'd known you were coming to see me. Why don't we suspend this until I've had time to look it over."

He still spoke to the window. "What help Kate needs can come from her teacher. I know I'm being rude, but frankly, I've had a lifetime of school psychologists, social workers and well-meaning analysts poking into the lives of my family. We're unconventional, Dr. Hollins, but we're survivors, as most people in town can tell you on the off chance you don't already know. My brothers and I thrived in an atmosphere far less supportive than Kate's."

"Mr. Branigan, I have no intention of going to people in Millbrook for information on your family. I'm only concerned about Kate and her relationship with you and her mother. Obviously I could make an appointment with Mrs. Branigan by herself, but if the two of you were agreeable, it might be better to meet together—for Kate's sake. If that's not possible, of course I'm happy to meet separately. I never meant to offend you. You're entitled to your privacy. You all are." She looked again at his wedding band and the signature on the detention slip. "This is signed by Holly Bancroft Branigan. Would that be Kate's mother or stepmother?"

Sean weighed the moment. "Kate's not the only one in need of some tutoring and homework. You're in need of both."

"Mr. Branigan?"

"The girls have lost their mother. My wife died four years ago of a congenital aneurysm."

She blanched. "I'm terribly sorry. No one told me. Surely you can understand my mistake."

He ignored the pang of guilt. "I didn't think psychologists made mistakes. Holly's my sister-in-law. My daughters need a woman in their lives. They've developed strong relationships with all my sisters-in-law and their families, since Anne's death. It's what the girls want. I have to travel or work late shifts." Enough, he thought.

"How many are there?"

"I have five brothers. They're all married."

"My goodness. All in Millbrook?"

"Yes. Two have homes on the compound where we live, within walking distance for the girls. Kate and Suzy spend the majority of the time with them. The other three are close enough. Hell, one's even a pediatrician."

"Mr. Branigan, you don't need to give me any more explanation."

"You're right, I don't. Kate and her sister have boundaries, Dr. Hollins, and lots of structure. Kate's in the throes of puberty. These are tough years, but she has a flock of aunts who've been wonderful."

"I'm sorry. I didn't know your situation."

Something in him reveled in her contrite expression. "Well, now you do."

TWO

The following afternoon Julia left her office at three-thirty with time to kill until she met her son after his team practice at the high school. Cheers from the middle school soccer field that separated the building from the high school drew her attention and she immediately thought of Kate Branigan and her father. The girl's team was in a frenzy of hugs and whoops as a goal was scored. At the far edge of the field, a now-familiar figure stood with other parents and students, cheering on the players.

Well, now you do. Sean Branigan's terse remark had stayed with her through two long days of academic appointments and parent conferences. His fatigue, his reticence, even the inflection in his voice was still with her. She'd been called on the carpet for doing her job and for incompetence, a complicated combination.

Thoughts of Sean Branigan smothered everything else in her day.

Now, however, the man who had pointed out so painfully how ill-prepared and -informed she was, was grinning and cheering. The game or his enthusiasm or at least something other than her presence had transformed him. Even at a distance, it was easy to see that his brooding introspective qualities had vanished. He was buoyant. *Handsome* was the only word she could think of to describe him. Sean Branigan looked rested, happy, and handsome—uncommonly handsome.

Julia kept her distance despite her resolve to get back in touch with him, apologize and try again to make progress on behalf of his daughter. Their encounter had kept her awake, had affected her work.

As if he sensed that he was being watched, he turned to look across the crowd. Their eyes met. Incredibly green, impossible to forget. After barely a glance, however, he turned his attention back to the game as the action continued. His reaction was exactly what she had expected.

The unguarded moment made her stomach flip-flop. His rudeness made her hesitate. *Coward.* Both of them.

"They circle their wagons, those Branigans," Alfie Forbes had told her when they finally sat down to discuss Kate. "You can hardly blame them."

She didn't want to blame anyone. She wanted to apologize and this was as good a time as any. She walked toward the spectators and tried to convince herself it was all in his daughter's best interest.

"Mr. Branigan?" She waited until he turned. This time he smiled back at her. It was genuine and it thoroughly confused her.

"Yes?"

She smiled, too, buoyed by the change in him as she searched for an innocuous subject to open the conversation. "I see Kate out there. How's she doing?"

"Just great. Did you see that goal? She passed the ball right to center for a clear shot."

"She tells me soccer's her favorite sport."

"There's no doubt." He stopped as the ball streaked in Kate's direction and the teenager took it down the field, dodging and weaving. He cheered for her again and Julia paused to watch her make the important play.

She was astounded at how relaxed and animated Sean was. The tension and fatigue seemed to have melted. He'd either had a remarkable day or forgotten their conversation. But Sean Branigan didn't seem the type to forget much of anything. He stood now between the field and her line of vision.

She glanced at him surreptitiously, this widower with a family-support system any single parent would envy. She would have loved five siblings at her beck and call for Brett and Nick.

The breeze caught his hair and blew it off his forehead. He shaded his eyes with his hand. When the action slowed, he turned back to her. "I'm sorry. You were saying something about Kate."

"About you, actually. I'm afraid we got off on the wrong foot yesterday."

"Me?"

"At our conference in my office about Kate. My misunderstanding about her mother."

The smile again. He grinned and offered his hand. "I think you're confusing me with my twin brother. I'm Drew Branigan."

"Twin?"

"Identical."

"There's two of you?"

"Don't look so discouraged. You can only be the adjustment counselor Sean told me he lit into yesterday. You caught him on a bad day. He's all bark. Also sensitive as hell, overly protective since we lost Anne. Gave you a rough time yesterday, I gather. He's not one for therapy." Drew sighed. "Even now."

"I wasn't suggesting therapy." Julia stopped. More action in the game gave her the chance to catch her breath. She should have known that this vivacious person wasn't the man in her office. They shared the same height, the same green eyes and clear Black Irish complexion but there the similarities stopped. Sean Branigan was a shadow of his cheering, animated twin. It was as if Drew were the man his brother could be. Or might have been.

"Sean's in New Jersey till tomorrow, trying out some updated designs for harvesting equipment. South Jersey's in the midst of their harvest. Mostly dry picking down there, but a sizable group flood their bogs, too. I'm filling in for the cheering section."

"I gather you do that a lot, you and your wife."

"We all do."

"He's fortunate to have such support."

Drew nodded. "He's frazzled. Big job keeping the world at arm's length."

"Is he?"

"Lord, yes. Getting hauled into your office pointed out that he's not doing as perfectly as he'd hoped."

"I didn't haul him anywhere. Kate's history teacher had some concerns, that's all."

"Dr. Hollins, even if one of us initiates it, getting hauled into the school psychologist's office is the only way to describe a visit."

"That's unfortunate."

"Don't get defensive." He smiled. "Fate's a funny thing. Since we lost Anne, Sean's needed us more than we've needed him for the first time in his life. It's given most of my brothers a chance to pay him back." He grew pensive. "He'll have my hide for this, but you should know that Sean was the stable one. He married early, worked two sleep-robbing jobs for twenty years to help with tuition for Jody and Matt, the youngest of us. He and Anne were always safe haven when somebody needed to get away and blow off steam. He's done right by all his brothers. I'd guess part of his problem with you is the fact that he can't admit that he hasn't done as well with the girls."

"I never meant for any of you to think that, or to imply it to Sean. He's doing a fine job under very difficult circumstances. Drew, I'm afraid this is getting blown out of proportion. Growing pains on the part of a teenager is the norm, not the exception."

"You might mention that in your next appointment."

"We don't have one."

"Make one. He could use it and he sure as hell isn't going to call you." They were interrupted by the arrival of a woman and scampering children. "My wife, Holly." Drew touched each child on the shoulder. "Suzanne, Sean's youngest and mine, Maria." He put the emphasis on the first syllable. "And my son Peter. Shake hands, kids. This is Dr. Hollins."

"Whoa," came from Suzanne. "Are you the one who put Kate in detention?"

Julia leaned slightly and smiled. "Kate put herself there, I'm afraid. I'm just the one who talked with her. I think we worked everything out."

Maria looked up at her father. "She's the one you and Uncle Sean were fighting about."

Drew flushed, but the grin remained as he looked over his daughter to Julia. "As I said, Sean's not one for taking advice."

The game held their attention and Julia stayed until Nick arrived in the parking lot. As she excused herself, Drew shook her hand again. "Don't give up on him."

Julia frowned. "I think the problem's been exaggerated. It's only Kate and her schoolwork. I wasn't—"

"Sean's worth the effort."

Nick was drumming his fingers on the steering wheel of the family car in time to the rock music blaring from the car's tape player by the time she crossed the parking lot. She glanced at him, assessed his mood and slid onto the passenger seat. When she asked him to turn it down, he muttered a response but complied.

She asked about his day, received the usual one-word answer "fine," and stayed quiet. He continued to drum his fingers.

"You changed back into your school clothes."

"So."

"Nothing. You're usually in your shorts or sweats, that's all."

After a moment's hesitation, he turned on the ignition. "I didn't go to practice."

"Oh, Nick. Unexcused absences will keep you from playing."

"That's a joke. I never play anyway. Me and some guys were looking at a few cars this afternoon."

"Some guys and I," she corrected.

"Whatever. There's a bunch in great condition at a dealership in Plymouth. Dad thinks I should have my own car, too."

"It's been a long day, darling. Let's discuss something less volatile."

"Volatile? Jeez, Mom, I'm not asking for the moon."

"Did your father offer to pay for the car, or the insurance or the gas? We're in a small town now, Nick. Half the things any of us do are within walking distance."

"Nobody walks."

"You're adding to pollution when you don't."

"Give me a break, Mom. Look, I'll get a job. It'll pay for everything."

"Please, Nick, we've been through this so many times. It's all you can do with your sports. You're already involved in the Police League teen club on Saturdays and the Police League work—" Julia stopped and leaned back. It would take a concerted effort, but she was determined not to argue.

Nick followed the main road from the school grounds, past the medical center toward the streets of Millbrook proper. The hilly road flattened as it edged picturesque acres of cranberry bogs. The rectangular acres were crimson, foliage and berries nearly ready for the harvest, hemmed in on two sides by woodlots punctuated by the turning of sugar maples to orange and yellow, pressed up against the green of the spindly pines. She took the opportunity to change the subject.

"Aren't the bogs beautiful this time of year?"

Nick shrugged. "I guess so. Look, Mom, I already got a job."

She sat up. "We've discussed this."

"No, we haven't! *You've* discussed it. You've lectured and made me listen. Even if I don't get the car, I need the money. For college," he tried.

She smiled at the deliberate softening of his voice. "College."

"Sure, and music and clothes and stuff, so you don't always have to shell out money for me."

"But, Nick, a job—"

"It's only temporary. It's at the cranberry bogs. There's three locations. It's just through the harvest, then maybe some work in the winter, sanding and stuff. Just weekends. I got it through the League. One of the cops—well, he's not a cop anymore but he used to be—owns a ton of bogs and they always hire out this time of year."

Something tightened in Julia's chest. "One of the cops?"

"You know, the volunteer leaders. Ryan Branigan runs the shop class for the League guys who want to be mechanics. I went over last Saturday with him and he showed me around. Actually the Bittersweet Bogs are owned by his brother and sister-in-law. Ryan and three others own the other two. It's hard to keep it all straight. There's a ton of Branigans, but anyway they hired me."

"I've met two Branigans this week, one at the soccer game just now. Why didn't you mention this before?"

"Come on. You'd have said no in a minute." He glanced sideways. "I've been waiting for the right moment. Timing's everything, you always say."

"And now's the time to bring it up?"

He grinned. "I figured you'd be relieved, after thinking I almost bought a car."

"Wait a minute. You said you looked. You didn't say anything about buying."

"Just kidding."

"About the car, not the job."

"Right."

"Where, exactly, will you be working?"

"Wherever they need us. My grades are fine, Mom. It's only weekends. It's good money and safe and all that. Plus I liked the guys."

"The brothers of the fellow from the Police League?"

"Right. I'll actually be working for twins."

Inexplicably her heart began to pound. "That would be Drew and Sean."

"Whatever. They're Mr. Branigan and Mr. Branigan, to me."

Three

The following night at the Millbrook Lower School parent-teacher open house, Sean Branigan glared at his oldest brother. "Kevin, you're the one who's always telling me it's a gut thing. Well, my gut says no thanks."

"Loosen up, for heaven's sake. I was suggesting dinner or a movie, not an elopement." Kevin stuffed his hands into his pockets and rattled his car keys as his triplets' kindergarten teacher disappeared into the throng of parents.

Erin Branigan scowled at her husband. "Only a Branigan would call it a *gut* thing. It's a *heart* thing, you two, and if Sean says no, respect his feelings." She grinned at her brother-in-law. "You can't blame any of us for suggesting a date once in a while. I'd just as soon you didn't practice on the boys' teacher anyway. She has enough Branigans to deal with."

Kevin smirked. "He lives like a monk. It's not good for his—gut."

"I rest my case," Erin replied.

"I'd appreciate it if you both would give it a rest. Even if I were interested in her, or anyone else, this is a hell of a time of year to add that to my list of activities. You two would probably suggest I take her along on frost warnings to monitor the bogs all night."

"Worked for Ryan and Drew," Kevin replied.

"Kevin prefers warmer weather for hunkering down in the pine needles," Erin replied, despite the scowl from her husband.

"When and where and *if* I...hunker is none of your business," Sean said as a flash of familiar paisley scarf caught his eye. Julia Hollins passed and was cornered by a pair of anxious parents next to the bake-sale table. He grimaced at Erin's expectant expression. "Forget it. That's Dr. Hollins, Kate's adjustment counselor."

"The one Drew says you called on the carpet a few days ago?" Kevin asked.

"Is my life an open book?"

"It's been four years."

"Privacy is an unknown entity in this family."

"We're there for you," Erin whispered, grin in place.

Sean ignored them. Julia smiled and bent her head slightly as she spoke. Her body language was pure reassurance. The woman nodded. The man scribbled something in a notebook. Was their child guilty of flunking math? Cutting class? Sneaking cigarettes in the locker room?

Try as he might, Sean was unable to conjure up the irritation that had smothered his initial reaction to the brunette. For that he blamed his brother Ryan who had no idea what he'd unleashed when he'd mentioned hiring a teenager named Nick Hollins whose divorced mother had just moved him to Millbrook. Julia Hollins was single. He watched her as his heart pumped and his pulse pounded. Twice in two encounters with her—before he had time to shield himself with distrust, apprehension and skepticism—her presence had teased his overworked, unsuspecting body. A *gut thing,* he thought with disgust, grateful that Kevin and Erin had moved on to their children's classroom.

Julia's hair was piled in the same not-quite-prim style that accentuated her cheekbones and those all-seeing eyes. The industrial overhead lights dusted her crown with gold and auburn. He wondered how long it was. When, if ever, might she leave it loose? Mental images he didn't dare pursue flickered. Judging by the boys in her desk photographs, she had to be nearly his age. If she were approaching forty, she wore it very well.

She was wearing a red wool jersey scoop-necked sort of thing, fitted, demure, perfectly tasteful. The scarf—*that scarf*—lay draped again over her shoulder and along the curve of her breast. She shifted from one foot to the other and the paisley silk caught the light. Memory filled his head: her touch on his sleeve, her voice as she'd wakened him, the scarf, the sway of her breasts when he'd opened his eyes.

As she closed the conversation, Julia looked up and recognized him. There was a moment's hesitation before she smiled and started toward him. The old adrenaline surged. To his surprise, she cocked her head and looked him over almost playfully. It threw him further off balance. Those coffee-colored eyes were wide and clear, her glance as confident as always.

"Drew from the soccer game or Sean from my office?" She studied him and for a moment her smile flickered.

"Sean."

"Any other brothers here tonight?"

"Besides Drew? Kevin has triplets in kindergarten. Look, Dr. Hollins—"

"Am I being too personal again? Forgive me. I just wanted to make amends for the other day. We got off to a rough start. It was only Kate's well-being I was thinking of. We both want what's best for her. I hope you've accepted that by now."

"There are some things I'll accept and some I won't."

"The tutoring?"

"She's willing to give it a try."

"And how about some guidelines for your brothers, so she has the same rules wherever she is." She touched her scarf.

"We have guidelines. I'll admit you gave me some things to think about, but strong family support is already in place." He realized he'd been staring. "Sorry. That's the scarf you were wearing in your office the other day."

"Yes, I guess it is." She smiled. "I'm sorry about that encounter and I apologize for my ignorance. You're recalcitrant, Sean Branigan. Understandable, I suppose. Not hopeless, though, far from hopeless."

The bustle around them had forced them together, close enough so that he could see the steady beat of her pulse at her temple. "I want what's best for my daughters."

"I never thought otherwise."

"Just as I'm sure you want what's best for your sons."

Her dark eyes widened at his remark. Her soft, rapid breathing surprised him. "My sons?"

"My brother hired one of them to work at the bogs during the harvest. Nick, is it?"

She glanced at the bustle around her. "Yes. Nick."

"If you're looking for an excuse to examine Kate's home life, say so."

Julia blanched and then flushed, cheekbone to temple. Her eyes flashed and the scarf slid. Her breasts, taut against the wool, heaved as she straightened her spine. "Are you suggesting that I'd use my children as a ploy? Do I really appear that devious?"

"Nick Hollins joins Ryan's Police League group, applies for work during the harvest at the exact time that his mother the adjustment counselor puts my daughter and our lives under her microscope. Is it coincidence?"

"Of course it is. Nick took the job without even telling me. I've agreed, but initially I didn't want him working for you or anyone. He already has a full schedule with soccer and the Police League. If he's mentioned Ryan's name, through the league, I never made the connection." She lowered her voice until he had to lean forward. "I'm sorry you're suspicious and mistrusting but you're dead, flat wrong about me."

"Then I apologize."

She narrowed her gaze. "Just like that?"

"I can admit when I'm wrong."

"How refreshing. Maybe you are Drew."

"Look—"

"Poor humor. I apologize. You are wrong, very, in this case. I think we both need some breathing room, literally and figuratively. You're a complex man, Sean, infuriating and exhausting, too."

"Can't stand the same scrutiny you're giving me?"

"My concerns are purely professional. Yours are purely defensive and vindictive. If you'll excuse me, I have other parents I need to talk to."

"Just as well."

She cocked her head and adjusted her scarf as her composure returned, but stayed silent. Sean turned his back and swallowed his guilt as she worked her way toward the door. She hadn't mentioned her sons; hadn't mentioned that she was a single parent with an ex-husband who used child support as a bargaining tool to manipulate her. She hadn't mentioned that she'd enrolled Nick in the Police League program, in her search for some positive male role models. Ryan Branigan put aside a weekend a month to work with the boys.

Despite his accusation, Sean believed Nick Hollins had wound up under the Branigan wing by coincidence. He also believed, however, that keeping Julia Hollins on the defensive would give him some desperately needed breathing room. She may not have done her homework where the Branigans were concerned, but where Hollinses were concerned, Sean had done his. It deepened his guilt.

The psychologist had her own battles to wage. It piqued his curiosity. The fact that her parenting skills might be as strained as his dissolved her invincibility.

Julia Hollins was suddenly vulnerable. Color in her own cheeks, her abrupt departure confirmed it.

He'd thought the confrontation would give him leverage. Instead, deep and steady as his own heartbeat, something still unrecognized began to form in him. A flush crept through his complexion as she moved away. Pleasure teased, sent his pulse to his ears and blood to his groin. He flushed with the shock of its intensity and turned abruptly to the PTA calendars for sale on the table.

Four

The floodlights at the corner of the barn cast long, black shadows over the courtyard as Julia watched Sean Branigan swallow his surprise. His brother Ryan made the introductions. "This is Nick Hollins, Sean, and his mother Julia. She says you've met."

"Dr. Hollins."

"Julia, please." Her breath came in soft, gray puffs. "Ryan swung by to pick up Nick and asked if I might like a tour since I was still awake. I'm curious to see what you men lose sleep over."

"Turns out Julia and Nick live in the village, too, behind Sky and me on Penham Road," Ryan added.

"How convenient. It's too cold for chatter. Let's get going." With a swing of his flashlight, Sean led the group from the cobbled courtyard. A trim vegetable garden framed in picket fencing delineated the lawn and private area of the original Branigan homestead.

Just beyond, the land sloped into a ten-foot sand pile and down to the cart path, which led to the flat rectangular acres in which the cranberries grew. The rutted path ran along the easterly edge, which stretched out under the stars to the dark shape of woods that formed the farthest boundary.

The night was clear with a sliver of moon suspended over the group. It was after midnight, still and cold, and Julia slapped her hands against her jacket as the brothers began their monitoring.

They followed the cart path, past the mound. Sean cast the flashlight beam on it and explained the need to sand the bogs every third or fourth year. In front of her the acres leveled out, bog acres delineated by dikes and the dark outline of the pump house which drew water from a pond and was now distributing it through the underground sprinkler system over the ripening crop. A golden retriever trotted among them, obviously partial to Sean.

Over the soft *whoosh* of the irrigation system, he petted the dog and explained the need to monitor and spray when frost was threatening to keep the berries from freezing. Ryan beamed his flashlight into the mass of cranberry bushes. Pump house, sprinkler heads, saddle system . . . the man was engrossed in his explanation and for once Nick seemed enthralled.

"Sixty-five gallons, per acre, per minute," her son repeated.

"Just to hold the crop to maturity. A hard frost could wipe them out overnight," Ryan added.

"But they're nearly ripe."

"And fragile. If they freeze and burst on the vine, they're no good."

The four of them stood on the dike that edged the cultivated acres. Sean aimed the light on the pump house, then the adjoining pond. She watched him longer than was proper, longer than was good for her respiratory system. He had on chinos and hiking boots and a jacket open to his breastbone over a thick wool sweater. His dark hair was hidden under a watch cap snug and trim around his handsome features. Watching him here, on his own land, even in the dark, intensified the sense of self-containment and independence he protected so fiercely. Kate and Suzanne Branigan were in excellent hands.

Across the pond a third house stood alone at the edge of the pines. There were just the stars, no city lights, and illumination spilled from the kitchen and family room windows out onto the shadowed lawn. The handsome New England saltbox was a century newer than the two behind her on the hill, back by the barn.

She wondered which of the houses the girls were in, which house was Sean's. She didn't bother to guess. She hadn't been correct about much where any Branigan was concerned, except the irritation Sean had made no effort to hide when she'd slid from the passenger seat of Ryan's four-wheel-drive vehicle twenty minutes earlier.

A hand on her shoulder made her jump. "They're sound asleep up the hill at Drew's."

"You still think that I'm on some social-service mission?"

"Why else would you come all the way out here after midnight and freeze your fingers off watching us put Nick through his paces?"

"Isn't it obvious? You're such wonderful company, I couldn't resist Ryan's invitation." She shook her head. "Forgive my sarcasm, but will it always be this awkward every time we face each other after yet another confrontation?"

"Nothing's awkward but having to work with a woman along."

"I was still up when Ryan drove over to pick up Nick. He thought I might like to see how things work. It gave me a chance to try and convince you again that you're far too suspicious."

"It's my nature."

"Understandable, but wrong. Could we get back to the bogs? They're really quite impressive."

"You can't be too impressed. Ryan and Nick are headed for Drew and Holly's acres already. They're halfway to the barn. You didn't even know we'd finished with these."

"I was admiring the house. Which brother's is it?"

"Mine." He was silent for a moment, then whistled for the retriever and started along the dike, forcing her to catch up. "When the girls are there, I never monitor anything but these bogs and Bittersweet, up the hill. Kevin and Drew split the bogs out on the Duxbury Road and the Taft acres. Jody rotates with all of us. Matt's rarely involved. He's the doctor."

"You don't owe me any explanation."

"Your profession says otherwise. This time of year during the night, we're apt to be up for hours. The girls are more comfortable at one of my brothers' where there are women present. Kevin's house is there by the barn, Drew's up the hill."

"Where Ryan says you all grew up."

"Yes."

Even when Drew had mentioned the death of Sean's wife he had used the first person. When *we* lost Anne; *our* loss. She squinted in the dark at the family compound. Rarely had she run into such family unity.

She tried to feel her way through a safe topic, which was as difficult as walking the rutted path in the dark. "Lovely dog."

"Puck."

"Midsummer Night's Dream?"

"Anne had just gone back to teaching English when she died. The puppy was the O'Connor sisters' idea, for Kate and Suzy."

"O'Connor?"

"Kevin, Jody and Matthew are married to sisters. They lost their mother as kids, too."

"You really are a tight group."

"Used to be all bachelors and dogs, now it's kids and dogs. Max and Domino before Puck. They lived at the main house—Kevin's now that we're all on our own."

"I didn't realize Ryan and his family live right in the Millbrook Historic District. Theirs is the Joshua Schuyler House."

"Sky is Jane Schuyler. It was in her family. A bit high style for Ryan but he likes living in the village. He needs the breathing room."

They skirted the edge of the sand pile. Nick and Ryan were passing through the floodlit courtyard. Julia stopped. She put her hand on Sean's jacket sleeve. "I didn't come out here to spy, or check up or do anything official."

"Your idea of a fun evening?"

"Yes. I thought it might be."

"Dr. Hollins—Julia—I don't believe it and, frankly, I don't need this. You've put my family under enough scrutiny."

"You're mistaken. I had no idea whether you'd be out here tonight or not, but I did hope that if I ran into you, I might see another side to Sean Branigan, someone less defensive on his own turf. I'm sorry I was wrong." She paused. "Don't be so hard on yourself. Maybe that way you won't be so hard on the rest of us."

When he didn't respond, she dropped her hand and turned, starting out after Nick and Ryan, who were casting their flashlight beams ahead of them as they approached the second set of bogs on the Branigan homestead. She stumbled after them in the dark, past Kevin and Erin's rambling country house and imagined it full of six rambunctious orphaned boys and their dogs.

She shouldn't have come. Whatever it was that kept her heart thumping and sleep sporadic had nothing to do with an eighth grader who missed homework assignments and challenged her teachers. It had even less to do with the restless son she'd used as an excuse to wangle a midnight invitation to the Branigan bogs. It had to do with a man at odds with himself, his life and the role she was playing in it. She had no way of knowing whether his motivation was still grief, simple Irish stubbornness or Yankee suspicion of newcomers. Whatever it was, it exhausted her.

"Look, I'm sorry."

Julia turned as Sean materialized next to her. She continued to walk, however, over the lawn separating Kevin's homestead from Drew's. "My fault. I press. It's my nature."

"I guess we could use a little of it now and then."

"We?"

"Katie and me. Suzanne, too, if she ever starts a fire in the locker room."

"Humor?"

He sighed and stopped.

She stopped, too. In the dark, geese honked somewhere over the pines. "It's incredibly beautiful, you know. The sand hills and the woods running to the bogs. Every once in a while I see a glimmer of birch." She pointed. "Like over there, just the moonlight and the sharp white bark peeking out from the woods. Kind of the way I see a glimmer of something in you. Humor, maybe, or maybe just friendliness peeking out from that gruff hidebound exterior."

"Hidebound?"

"Tough as old shoe leather. Damned if the man doesn't smile." He did, reluctantly, and when she caught him at it, he bent to his dog and ruffled his fur.

"Beautiful out here, as I was saying. I'm sure Nick's thinking this is a great spot for romance. I suppose you take it for granted."

His expression changed, but there wasn't enough light to read it. "Julia, I take very little for granted."

In the four crop seasons since Anne's death, Sean had never been out here with a woman. The romance of the bogs, in and out of season, was his bachelor brothers' domain. He'd had Annie, always. She'd been reliable, comfortable and the one light in his life when he'd lost his parents as a teenager.

He'd never been like the others, at loose ends, defiant like Ryan, academic like Jody and Matt. Anne had put his life in order and given him a focus. His love for her was based as much on gratitude and comfort as it had been on passion.

"It was my brothers who were out here," he murmured, absorbed in his own thoughts.

"Your brothers?"

He shrugged. "Sorry."

"I'm interested."

"Never mind." Women and the bogs: he wasn't about to delve into that subject. The night air and shadows had transformed the one who stood looking up at him. She was on foreign soil and her self-assurance had ebbed. Fine with him, except for the damned feeling that he should apologize or spill his guts or open his heart.

She was dressed for the weather in corduroy slacks, hiking boots and a teal green fleece jacket with a ski hat over her hair. She opened her jacket and his skin prickled as though she'd touched him. All he could think about was her scarf, the stupid drape of the stupid scarf over curves and softness he had no business recalling. Blood began to surge in places he dared not consider and he wished at that moment he were half as hidebound as she thought.

Try as he might, and he'd devoted hours to it, he couldn't tap the source of this unrequited desire. The moment he came within shouting distance of Julia Hollins, his body took on a life of its own. Sixteen-year-olds wrestled with this, not forty-two-year-olds. His adrenaline went haywire, his face burned. She was a constant reminder of the gaping hole in his life.

They reached Bittersweet Bogs and he squatted deliberately and shone his light on a set of sprinklers he knew were working perfectly. He stared at droplets clinging to the vines: a million diamonds under the autumn night. His hand shook.

"Sean?" She knelt next to him and the ache was as deep as the pleasure.

"Have to check each one."

Women and the bogs, integral parts of his brothers' lives. Most were now wives, and even the three who were sisters were as different from each other as the brothers they loved. Through it all, he'd been the steady, settled one. He listened to their stories, some humorous, some passionate. There were summer heat waves, winter snows, harvest moons and dewy-eyed, overheated couples ripe for the seduction of the pine and birch woods, the apple orchard, or the golf course. Each rimmed a different set of Branigan properties. Abruptly he stood.

"Yes?"

"Nothing." He chuckled in spite of himself. "We'd better catch up to Ryan and your son."

"That couldn't have been a laugh. Only your brothers do that."

"You haven't given me much to laugh about."

"Me?" She stopped.

"You and your analysis."

"Then I apologize. Laughing becomes you. You should do it more often."

"I'll try to remember that."

"This seems a lovely place to raise children."

Sean stopped abruptly. "Damn it, Julia, I love them. You can't have any doubt about that. I've been gone so much that I'm no good with them, that's all. Holly and Erin understand the girls. Kate and Suzanne need women right now. I love them but I can't give them what they need."

"You are a major part of what they need."

"Half the time when they're with me, we're like strangers." He stared at her. "You've been waiting for me to spill my guts and there it is."

"Once again you're being awfully hard on yourself. Puberty's a double-edged sword. It makes the child incredibly self-centered as his or her body changes and hormones kick in, but it's also the beginning of the need for separation from a parent. Both are a necessary part of growing into an independent adult. Try to remember. Surely you felt that way." She stopped and shook her head. "Forgive me."

"My separation was real and permanent. I never had the luxury of yearning for independence from my parents. It was dumped on me. My brothers and I made it through that and my daughters and I will make it through this. The system we've worked out is fine. Branigans take care of their own. Kate and Suzanne have exactly what they need right up that hill."

"You're angry that I came out here tonight. I'm sorry."

He didn't deny it.

"This is your home. It's not the same as seeing you in my office. I understand that, Sean. It was presumptuous of me. If I had the car, I'd drive myself home."

"We'll be finished soon." They continued along the dike as Ryan and Nick did the same on the other side.

"What were you chuckling about a minute ago?"

"It's not appropriate for a school counselor."

"How about for a friend? Was it something to do with these bogs?"

"You're not a friend."

His remark stopped her in her tracks. "I'm not the enemy."

Guilt softened him, but desire teased, kept his pulse strong. A flush rose from his turtleneck. "You mentioned romance. You're right. My brothers spent a healthy amount of time out here on their dates. That's all I was thinking about."

Julia turned the flashlight beam on him. "Juicy stories?"

"Branigans are given to flushing," he muttered as he pushed the light away.

"Endearing," she said. "Drains some of the stubbornness out of you."

They reached the orchard that edged Bittersweet Bogs. She pulled off her cap and tendrils slipped from her topknot. How long had it been since he'd touched a woman's hair, felt the strands in his fingers, smelled a familiar shampoo?

"Whether you tell me or not and whether my coming here tonight was appropriate or not, I'm glad I came. It's a nice way to get to know Kate and her family."

Sean watched the stars. In four years, grief had dissipated into an ache that had dogged him until that, too, wore itself out. He was left hollow, a loneliness exacerbated by the flight of his daughters, despite the hope that they were getting what they needed.

Julia's arm pressed lightly against his as she spoke. He imagined her, not in bed, not in his arms, but fresh from a shower, towel-drying her hair, which smelled as it did now. The intimacy and spontaneity of the image shocked him into coughing.

The sound of his name split the night as Ryan called him. Sand in the sprinkler heads, a broken joint, whatever it was, he welcomed the diversion and headed for his brother and Julia's son.

This third encounter with the doe-eyed, statuesque adjustment counselor stunned him. His hollowness opened like an abyss. He ached to fill it and fought the need even as he left her on the dike. *A gut thing,* he thought ruefully, a physical, instinctive gut thing for a woman who read his emotions as easily as he read the Sunday papers.

No fires he'd ever fought in his career equaled the heat of the one he fought in himself. Not now, he thought, not after all this time. Not her. Julia Hollins's motives were as transparent as the thin glaze that frosted the banks of his family bogs.

"But Uncle Drew already said I could go."

"Suzanne, I was going to take you and Kate to a movie tonight."

"But I've already been invited. I want to go with my friends. I already got permission."

"You should have asked me."

"I was up the hill when they called. That's not my fault. You were in New Jersey or someplace. Uncle Drew already said..."

"I know, I know. All right, but next time, get permission from me."

With a hurried promise, Suzanne grabbed her jacket. "See you at the bogs."

Sean stuffed his breakfast dishes into the dishwasher as he counted to ten and turned to Kate, equally impatient with him.

"You can't make me do this every stupid year."

"You're part of the family. This is tradition, Kate."

"I'm sorry I came over here for my jeans. I don't
care about Suzanne. The only tradition is for me to
baby-sit everybody. I don't have one cousin my age.
All I do is run around and keep everybody else from
falling in the bogs or getting near the sand pile. It's not
as if I even get to help. I hate it. I'm not going!"

Sean smiled.

"Stop laughing at me! It's not funny. Nothing in
this stupid family is funny. I mean it, I wish I'd had
my jeans at Aunt Holly's."

He put out his hand, but stopped. "I wasn't laughing. I was admiring you, sweetheart. You look so
much like your mother when you get all steamed up."

"If she were here, she'd understand. She wouldn't
make me go to the stupid harvest. And don't call me
'sweetheart.' It's a baby name. You know I hate it."

"I'm sorry. I keep forgetting. As for your mother,
she never missed one, even when I was at the fire station." Sean sighed as Kate stomped from the room. As
rock music blared from the second floor, he consid-
ered his options: dictator, arbitrator, father, friend.
The feisty redhead with fire in her eyes wanted none
of them.

Julia Hollins was right. The Kate he had cherished
since the moment of her birth had evaporated. Some
alien creature, all temper and tears, had taken over
when he wasn't looking. The only thing that gave him
hope was the fact that most of the time this alien didn't
seem to like herself any better than he did.

Sean finished his coffee and laced up his work
boots, then followed the music to its source. Her door
was open and Kate was lying on her rarely used bed,
staring at the ceiling.

He knocked on the door frame. "I've come up with a compromise."

"Why do you always have to come into my room?"

He pointed to his feet as he leaned over the threshold. "First, because that's where you are. Second, I'm still in neutral territory, if you'd care to look."

"Everything's a joke with you."

Another sigh. "Nothing that has anything to do with my children is a joke. Believe it or not, I take your feelings very seriously."

"Then why can't—"

"Even when I don't agree."

"You're so unfair."

"Parents are, sometimes. Kate, believe it or not, I love being your father."

"Sure. That's why I hardly see you."

"Is that how it feels?"

She shrugged. "I know how things are. I know about your jobs and everything. Just forget it."

"No. It's obviously important."

"If Suzy and I were boys, would we still live with the others?"

Sean paused, torn between the need to get to the bogs and the need to address Kate's question. "I'd still want to make sure you were safe and cared for when I couldn't be here."

"Dr. Hollins said you'd say that."

"You've talked about this with her?"

"Once in a while. I've spent some time doing homework in her office. She pretends she's all busy, but she's really waiting for me to spill my guts."

Sean suppressed a smile. "And do you, spill your guts, I mean?"

"No. I talked about the smoking thing. Courtney Santos thinks she's so incredibly awesome when she smokes you'd have lighted up in the locker room, too, just to show her how stupid she is."

"And what about Drew and Holly's? Have you changed your mind about staying there so much?"

"No. It's just that Suzy and I are there a lot, even when you're here."

"You wanted it that way."

She nodded.

"Kate?"

"No, I do, really. It's fine."

"Are you sure there's not more to this?"

"Yes. I don't like this house much anymore anyway. When I'm here it just reminds me of all the stuff I can't change."

"Happy memories, too, you always said."

"I know, but at Aunt Holly's it's different. I don't have to think about that stuff all the time." She sat up. "Look, don't we have to go, or something?"

"Yes, and I've come up with a compromise for today. No baby-sitting. I'll find real work for you."

She finally looked at him. "Cranberry work? Can I wear waders?"

"You'd better."

"You'll put me in the bogs?"

"In the bogs, in waders. Why don't we get up the hill and see what's needed? We've got some extra help. Ryan hired one of his League boys, Nick Hollins. Dr. Hollins's son, as a matter of fact."

"Just what I need."

"He'll be working and learning, too. This might be the day to get you on the eggbeaters."

"You always said I was too young."

"Maybe I was wrong."

"You, wrong? That'll be the day." Despite her sarcasm, her mood brightened as she sat up.

Five

Bittersweet Bogs were ready. The six acres that bordered Drew and Holly's house had been flooded and lay waiting for the Branigan brothers to begin the harvest. In typical New England fashion, the threatened freeze of the night before had been replaced by nearly balmy weather. The day was warm, and free of all but the occasional cloud. By the time Sean and Kate arrived, the property was humming with activity.

Kate pointed to the children scattered on the lawn that ran down to the dike. "See? A zillion cousins all waiting for me to baby-sit."

"At last count there were twelve, and nobody's waiting for you, sweetheart." He cringed at his use of her pet name. "Sorry. I'll try to remember."

Kate shrugged. "It's okay, I guess. It's just sometimes it really bugs me. Thanks for asking Uncle Drew if I can help on the eggbeater. I never thought he'd agree even though you guys were probably babies when you started riding around on them.''

''You're right. I harvested my first bog before I started kindergarten.''

''Very funny.'' Suddenly she narrowed her gaze. Ryan's wife, Sky, was walking down the hill with her toddler by the hand and infant daughter in a backpack. The woman with her bent to pick up a dropped rattle. ''So that's why you wanted me out here,'' Kate cried.

Sean shook his head. ''I told you, no baby-sitting.'' Julia Hollins stood and gave the toy back to the baby as Sean's heart thundered.

Kate glared at her father. ''You wanted me out here so Dr. Hollins could pick my brain. You said her son would be here, not her. I practically live in her office already. Isn't detention enough? What a sneaky thing to do.''

''Kate, go get to work. Drew's waiting for you. I'm sure Dr. Hollins didn't come to see you.'' As his daughter crossed to Drew and the heavy equipment, Sean met Julia's glance. He called up enough anger to clench his jaw, but desire nearly smothered it. He was already aware of the flush in his cheeks.

Julia waved. She had on a turtleneck sweater and jeans with a Windbreaker tied around her waist, and she approached him the minute she broke away from Sky and the children. Her breasts jostled as she maneuvered the hill. Ample breasts; the woman had a figure that wouldn't quit. He was tempted to hand her his jacket. He hadn't been fixated on female anatomy since his own puberty.

"Ryan and Sky invited me to tag along to see how all this works. Your brother said something about the bogs being big enough for both of us and that you'd be so busy I'd hardly be noticed."

Hardly be noticed. Sean glared across half an acre at his middle brother, who was busy lifting his baby daughter from Sky's backpack.

"I'll stay clear of your branch of the family. I don't intend to interfere."

"You are, no matter what your intentions. It's one of your many talents."

Her demeanor changed. "Have I been such an intrusion?"

"In my life is one thing, but Kate's is off-limits, off school grounds. Yes, to answer you. You put her on the defensive. Julia, you can understand that it's tough enough at school without your showing up here on her weekend."

"Kate." She sighed. "I certainly didn't come to spy on her. She mustn't think that. She's a terrific girl. You should be very proud of her."

"You could have found that out at school."

"And instead I wangle another invitation out here from your brother? I've only offered a few suggestions, which might help you and your daughters if you weren't so obdurate, intractable and recalcitrant."

"Any other ten-dollar words you want to spit out at me?"

"A few four-letter words come to mind."

"Try them. I'd love to hear you swear."

"Change my image?"

"Maybe. I told you last night what our arrangement is. How much more do you need to see? How many more stories do you need to hear? This is my family, all of it—five brothers, five sisters-in-law, ten nieces and nephews. I had a strong eighteen-year marriage, which has been over for four years. Anne's brother and his family live in Sturbridge. Her sister's in Portsmouth. Her parents have retired to Hilton Head. Life goes on."

Julia cringed at the change in his voice. It wasn't despair, or grief. The edge, the tone, were closer to resentment. As Kevin called to Sean, she added hastily, "I'm sorry you see this as some sort of invasion."

"After last night I shouldn't be surprised."

"I'll go. I probably should. Can someone drive me back to Millbrook?"

"You're here. You might as well stay. Don't argue. If you go, I'll be blamed for driving you away. I don't need five dog-tired cranberry growers growling at me."

"They think there might be some merit in my advice?"

"I didn't say that."

"But they might?"

"I haven't asked and they haven't offered opinions. I'd like to keep them out of this. Stay. With all these kids, we could use the extra hands and eyes. Just give Kate breathing room."

"I'll speak to her only long enough to make it clear I'm here socially." They exchanged a glance. "Sean, if you must know, I came as much for Nick as myself."

"Nick? He's sixteen. We run a safe, tight ship."

"Safety isn't my concern. He's at loose ends with himself. His brother's off at college, new friends, new demands."

"Give the kid some breathing room, too. Let him discover who he is and what he's capable of." Sean adjusted his waders. "Forget I said that, it makes me sound like a psychologist. If you take the advice, it'll just make you concentrate more on my kids." He snapped his shoulder straps over his sweater and left for the bogs.

Julia approached Kate, who stood by herself at the dike, adjusting her own waders. She was watching Ryan, knee-deep in the first set of bogs, instructing Nick and others in his Police League group in the use of the wooden floats used to corral the floating berries.

"I hope you'll give my son some pointers. Nick Hollins, the one in the red sweater."

"Me?"

"He's new to this."

Out in front of them, Drew Branigan drove the wide, flat water reel off the flatbed truck and into the second set of flooded acreage.

"So that's an eggbeater," she said.

"Yeah. It knocks the ripe berries off the vines without hurting them. My dad worked on the design of that one. He went out to Wisconsin and met with other growers out there. Dad says I'm old enough to drive it with Uncle Drew, even though we're at Bittersweet."

"Even though?"

"When they do these bogs, it's a tradition for the whole family to come out and have a picnic and stuff. Somebody always takes pictures. They're all over Uncle Kevin's great room and in the office. They go back to when my grandparents were still alive."

"How nice."

"Not really. I hate being the oldest. Till now at Bittersweet I had to help watch out for all my cousins.

Every year there's new babies, so a lot of my aunts can't help. If it's a year for sanding, somebody drops a pile here from the big one down the hill and you have to keep everybody off. Have you ever tried to keep a little kid out of playing in a sand pile?''

"Tough?''

"Yeah. You have to keep them away from the dikes. Somebody could fall in . . . or out.''

"Out?''

"Last year Kip fell out of one of these apple trees and broke his collarbone. I dared him to climb it, so of course I got blamed. Uncle Matt's a doctor so he had to stop working and go with Aunt Erin to the hospital. Everybody was really mad.''

Julia smiled. "Being the oldest comes with a lot of responsibility.''

"Being the oldest is a total pain.''

"It must have some advantages. I don't see any of your cousins getting to help on the eggbeater.''

"Dad finally says I'm old enough to do real stuff. Nick will too, probably.'' Her endearing flush was reminiscent of her father's. "So he's your son.''

"Yup. That's why I'm here,'' she added conspiratorially. "To make sure everything goes all right.''

"You're spying on him? You and my dad have a lot in common. He sends all my relatives everywhere I go, practically. Uncle Ryan's pretty cool. He does a good job with his guys. You can chill about Nick.''

Julia watched Sean's distant figure until she was aware that Kate was watching her. "Thanks. I'll try to. Your dad puts a lot of faith in you.''

"I know. Don't bother with the lecture about not letting him down. Everybody else gives me that one.''

"I can't imagine that you ever let your dad down.''

"Right. You try explaining a fire in the locker room when your dad's a fire fighter and don't forget I flunked my history test last week."

"Kate, your dad knows how the fire started. He also knows you're struggling with schoolwork. There's help available."

"You're not kidding there's help. He has the school shrink show up practically at my house so I won't be embarrassed at school."

"I told you, I came for Nick."

"Come on, Dr. Hollins. I know why you're really here."

Six

Sean or no Sean, Julia decided to stay. Two hours later she excused herself from Sky, Erin and the children who stood around the small campfire watching the kindling snap. *I know why you're really here.* The child's perception had kept her off-balance for the rest of the morning.

The sun was high and the temperature comfortable. Nick, Kate and other family members were corralling the last of the berries in the first bog while Kevin and Drew moved the water reel to the third grid. She walked deep into the orchard and leaned against a knarled tree, heavy with fruit.

The day's conversations had included Sky's explanation of the Branigan men, from orphaned teenagers through the death of Sean's wife. The perspective only added to her confusion.

"Hiding so no one'll put you to work?"

She jumped. Sean was standing between the trees. He came toward her and tossed an apple core into the flooded bog.

"I thought you were out there with your brothers," she replied.

"Minor rake repair. I'm on my way back."

"I decided to stay. To keep you blameless, you understand."

"I get blamed for enough around here."

"I wanted to convince Kate that I didn't come to spy on her. I think I also need to convince her father."

He played with the rake. "I'm sorry I gave you such a hard time this morning. I know you people mean well. I just don't want my kids subjected to the scrutiny I went through—we all went through."

"Sky talked about that today, your background, the struggles."

"I'm not crazy about that, either."

"Don't be too hard on her. She filled in lots of gaps. It makes things a lot more understandable. Your entire family seems eager to apologize on your behalf." He swore and she ignored it. "You should have given me the details last night."

"Julia, somehow you get right inside my head even when I don't give you details."

"A compliment?"

"A quandary. I don't know how the hell you do it, but I wind up feeling as though I spilled my entire life to you. It isn't comfortable."

"This isn't twenty-five years ago and I'm not some state-appointed psychologist, nor am I making value judgments about your parenting skills."

"Kate and Suzy do enough of that."

"And Nick's never had a problem telling me what kind of a mother I am."

"A damn good one. How could you not be?"

"Thank you. I'm no stranger to how tough it is raising children of the opposite sex alone. It gives them every excuse in the book to shout, 'You can't possibly know how I feel.'"

"Kate's line is, 'It's a girl thing.' Hell of it is, she's right most of the time."

"Don't be so sure. Kids'll use any excuse that works to separate themselves from authority. I know life's given you some awful kicks in the ribs, but you're a survivor. You have a wonderful life and a great family."

The day was beautiful. Sunlight filtered through the apple trees and left bright green patches in the October grass. A breeze rippled the water and lifted the leaves.

Sean nodded and looked out at the bogs. His pensive expression was familiar now. He retreated to a place she doubted anyone ever reached, except maybe Anne, certainly a place she was not meant to follow. When he finally spoke, he kept his focus on the bogs and his brothers. "I would have done anything to keep my daughters from the grief I went through."

"It doesn't make you less of a father because you couldn't."

"I hardly know them anymore, especially Kate."

Her heart jumped at his confession. "Sean, her mother would hardly know her, either. These are the years. She's transforming herself and being transformed, girl to woman." She smiled at his grimace. "It's called puberty, remember?"

"She's better off with Sky or Holly."

"Why better off?"

"They know her. They understand her."

"Keep her around more and you will, too."

"What if I can't?"

"Is that it? Fear of failure with your children? I'm sure your family adds to Kate's life. I know the women have the female perspective, but she needs her dad. She lost her mother and now she needs her father, maybe more than ever." She picked an apple. "This should wait for another time or you'll never believe my motives for coming out here, but Sean, you don't need to be so hard on yourself. Love works miracles, otherwise nobody would ever write songs and books and movies about it."

He smiled. "You and words."

"You and actions. Go back to work before your brothers start hollering. I'm keeping you."

He rubbed the rake handle and shifted it from one hand to the other. "You're keeping me from a lot more than my work. I can't sleep half the time. You make me suspicious and edgy and I wind up feeling as though I'm the one who should apologize. I swear I'm not going to say a word to you and I wind up talking your ear off. Damn if you don't tie me in knots."

"I'm trying to untie you."

"Maybe that's what this is."

"This?"

He pressed a fist to his chest. "The feeling of knots loosening." He turned suddenly and looked at her, hard, then leaned over. Without thinking, she closed her eyes. Adrenaline, desire, something instinctive made her part her lips. The elastic of her bra strained as she inhaled. Her breasts tightened, tingled over the steady pounding under her ribs.

For one excruciating moment, she wanted him to confess that what she'd been feeling since the first morning in her office was mutual, that this heady combination of desire and confusion was reciprocal, that the impossible was possible.

He put his finger on her bottom lip and rubbed slowly back and forth. She whimpered and caught her breath. Desire spiraled in every direction as heat beaded her breastbone with perspiration.

Sean touched her hair, then pulled back, well back, against an apple tree. There was no kiss. "I've never been so glad to be surrounded by family in my life. I should be arrested for what I'm thinking and I don't know what the hell I'm doing."

She flushed furiously as he stood looking at her. He had the greenest eyes she'd ever seen, with lashes thick enough to disguise emotion. "Maybe you're trying to convince yourself that I'm here after something other than Nick or Kate."

"Are you?"

The temptation to say yes, to throw caution and common sense out into the bogs, made her pant softly. She listened to the calls and cries of the children, the whine of the machinery. "I can't afford the luxury of self-indulgence."

"But if I'd continued just now?"

"Were you going to?"

"Would you have wanted me to?"

"You're answering a question with a question."

His smile was slow. "A lesson from the pro. I intend to leave them unanswered. I'm beginning to suspect that's the Hollins's approach to life."

"I think I should find a ride home, after all."

"Questions too close to the bone?" He closed his eyes.

"Answers might come too easily." She put her hand on his arm. "Thank you for what you've shared. It helps."

"With Kate, you mean."

"With Kate. With her father."

Sunday afternoon the Branigans finished Bittersweet Bogs with the help of Ryan's League members. Sean was at the wheel of the flatbed, parked on the cart path, with Nick beside him. Behind them, Drew and Kevin worked the water reel up the ramp for the return to the barn.

"So, Mr. Branigan, you think you could use me this week on the other bogs?"

"The ones down the hill will be flooded any day, end of the week at the latest. The Taft bogs have a while to go. I thought we only had you on weekends. Aren't you a soccer player at the high school?"

"I stink. It was Mom's idea. My brother was this big player at our old school. Millbrook's the state champ. I never was much good and I'm worse here."

"Hard to live up to your brother?"

"Brett's perfect."

"And Nick's not?"

"Hell—heck—not even close. Sorry."

"Strong feelings."

"Yeah, I guess so. I mean we get along great and everything, but he just kind of slides through life. No hassles."

"While your life's in turmoil."

Nick smiled. "Yeah, I guess so. I miss him, that's for sure. He took the edge off Mom."

"She cares a lot about you."

"I know."

"Do you ever think that one of the nice things about being new here is that nobody at the high school knows perfect Brett? You don't have to live up to anybody's reputation. Millbrook's just getting to know imperfect Nick on his own merit."

"You teasing?"

Sean grinned. "Millbrook's a good place to be yourself, Nick. If anybody can relate to your problems, the Branigans can. With six of us, one or another was always living up to somebody's expectations."

"Except the oldest. Kevin."

"Especially Kevin. He had to rise to the expectations of social workers, relatives, school counselors, you name it."

"Yeah, well, I've got a live-in school counselor breathing down my neck."

Sean watched him. Nick had his mother's strong features and thick dark hair. A head taller than Julia, he was a handsome strapping kid, bright, a willing worker whose interest in the mechanical aspects of the business had delighted Ryan. He had the same cautious way of looking at the world as most of the Branigans, which had already endeared him to the brothers.

"What's your dad have to say about soccer?"

"Win, win, win. Start over kid, be the best player in Millbrook. Make varsity and *I'll* even come to some games."

"I like a man who doesn't pressure his kids."

Nick laughed. "He thrives on it."

"He wasn't, by any chance, a crack soccer player himself?"

"Varsity in high school, varsity at Harvard."

"Aha, the fog's lifting."

"Fog?"

"Brett seems to be a perfect fit for his old man's shoes. Nick's foot's a different size."

"Dad's not so bad, just busy. He sort of has this other life now. He lives in Hartford."

"So your mother's the master of your fate at the moment."

"That's one way to put it."

"Can you explain what you want to her? If you quit the team, we'll sure see that you get the exercise. Your mother's a good listener."

"To everybody else, maybe."

"You, too, Nick, especially you."

Sean looked out into the orchard. Twenty feet from where they sat parked, he'd told Julia Hollins things he'd never confessed to his own family. Friday night he'd thought that's what she was after. She chipped away at his resentment; she inspired confidence where there should have been suspicion. It was a hell of a lot more than listening. It was emotional unlayering.

Julia stripped away pretense, saw through denial, laid bare doubts and fears until they seemed little more than shadows. She blew on embers buried in ashes until the heat was steady, the glow incessant. Sexual hunger, emotional need? He refused to put words to any of it. Saturday had turned him inside out, but it wasn't her behavior that haunted him.

It was his.

Seven

Monday afternoon and evening Sean taught a CPR refresher course, required regularly of all town personnel. Drew and Holly had insisted on making him dinner between sessions, pointing out that it would give him the chance to see his daughters, as well. He finished the first session at six-thirty, and by the time he arrived at his twin's antique farmhouse, the family had fallen into their evening routine.

Holly was at the kitchen table helping Peter with a science assignment. The girls were on the second floor. He climbed the stairs while Drew pulled supper from the refrigerator. Suzanne and Maria were lounging on the twin beds in the room they shared, boom box blaring. He greeted them, mentioned homework and reading, then knocked on the closed door of the guest room.

"I told you guys, I'm not hanging up yet."

"It's Dad."

He entered as she mumbled into the portable phone and stuffed it into the comforter. The teenager sat on the double bed with her legs crossed. Stuffed animals, many of which he recognized, sat on the pillows on either side of her and books lay open on the floor. Three posters of rock stars lined the wall behind her, as well as a collage of personal photographs, cut and pasted on shirt cardboard. What looked like a week's worth of clothing hung from the chair and the back of the open closet door.

He hadn't paid attention to how Kate had personalized the room, how many of her treasures lined the bookcase, how full the closet was. Julia Hollins's observations and admonitions made the detail clearer. It made him ache to have Kate and Suzanne home.

"Boy, I sure can tell who lives here," he managed.

"Yeah, well, it's easier than going back to the house for every little thing."

"Homework done?"

She shrugged. "Mostly." She rifled through her notebook and handed him a slip of paper. "Mrs. Forbes put my name in for a tutor from the high school, some honor student's supposed to call you."

"That should help."

"It beats grown-ups pestering and nagging me to death, but I don't need some high school kid telling me I can't add or subtract or that I don't know the Swedes settled Delaware."

"Very good."

"Yeah, well, I just read it. I'm fine. Really."

"You're a Branigan and you don't like to admit that you could use a little help now and then on the tough stuff. I know how you feel."

"Because Dr. Hollins was hanging around the bogs Saturday?"

Sean sat on the edge of the bed. "She didn't come to see you, Kate, but it's true that she wants to make sure you do well, that you get along in school. I have to agree with that. Maybe she could help with the tough stuff."

"Does she help you with the tough stuff? I mean stuff about me and all?"

"She wants me to be a good father."

"You're okay. You don't need some shrink telling you you're not."

"Sweetheart, Dr. Hollins isn't doing that. As a matter of fact, she was more concerned about Nick and how he's doing out there in the berries."

"He's awesome in the berries."

Sean grinned at her suddenly guarded expression. "Details?"

"Don't tease."

"I wasn't. He's struggling with soccer. Maybe you could practice with him. Give him some pointers."

"Right."

"So I'm not hopeless in the father department?"

"A lot of my friends have worse."

He laughed. "Is that a compliment?"

"Sure. Anyway my big worry isn't Dr. Hollins, it's Mrs. Forbes. She wants us all to think American history is to die for. She wants us to write colonial journals and pretend we're minutemen or Daughters of Liberty. I'm no good at that."

"So practice."

"I don't have time."

"You have the time. Make it a priority." He took the phone as she protested. "Study without being reminded. It keeps the grown-ups like Dr. Hollins and me from pestering and nagging you to death. Over here. At that desk. Come on, sweetheart." Over her complaints, he scooped up her books and laid them out on the desk top, ignoring the "Nick" drawn into the corner of her three-ring binder. He snapped on the study light and pulled out the chair.

"Get to it."

"Okay, okay."

"I love you, Kate."

"I know."

Suzanne was in the bathtub with a book report to finish when she got out. So Sean went back to the kitchen for dinner because he'd be leaving soon. Holly was now ministering to Peter's bath in the downstairs master bathroom. Sean took his dinner from the microwave oven as Drew pulled up a chair next to his brother.

"You're busy," Sean said. "I appreciate this. Kate and Suzy both have started to complain about the house."

"Yours?"

"Feels like only mine. Nobody else spends any time in it. Memories, I think."

"Four years, Sean. You've been in a sort of time warp holed up over there. The girls have gone on with their lives, just the way you wanted, just the way they had to. Redecorate or something. Shake things up over there. Get rid of the ghosts." Drew took a crouton from Sean's salad. "Julia Hollins seems to have a vested interest in your branch of the family. You might ask her opinion—for your daughters' sake, of course."

Sean glared. "You know why she's interested. Kate's history teacher sent up a warning flag. I met with the adjustment counselor. That's what they call them now. She's going to arrange for a tutor. That's all Julia Hollins is doing. The rest is coincidence."

"What rest?"

"Her son being part of Ryan's group, working for us, that stuff."

"Maybe. She shows up at Kate's soccer game, the bogs Friday night, then most of Saturday. Holly gave her a tour of the house, right down to the living arrangements for Kate and Suzy when they're here. All that professional interest made me nervous as hell at first." Drew laughed. "Till I got a good look at your complexion."

Sean stabbed a piece of potato. "All right, I admit I don't know what the hell to do with her."

"If she means to help, then listen. A little outside influence might be good for your soul. Good for the rest of you, too. Sparks are flying and heaven knows, twin brother, you could use a few in your life."

"No advice in the sparks department, thank you."

"Have you talked to her since the weekend?"

"No."

"Might not hurt."

"Then again it might."

Drew got up and poured a cup of coffee. "Care to elaborate?"

"She's in too much of my life, as it is. I need some breathing room."

"This is the nineties. I guess she's capable of calling you if she feels like it."

Sean sighed and followed his brother to the sink with his empty plate. "The nineties. I've been out of the loop so long I might as well be in the Dark Ages."

"Does that mean you're ready to stick your face out of the cave?"

"Give it a rest, Andrew."

"Give it some thought, Sean." The twins shared a clear, identical green-eyed glance.

Wednesday afternoon Nick was at the car as Julia left the school building. "No soccer practice?"

"I'm quitting."

"Nick, we've been through this."

"Don't start, okay? The coach hates me, I never play. I tried it for you and it didn't work. Just don't bug me about it." He got in and shut the door as she started the ignition. "I know I let you down. I know I'm not the star like Brett was."

"Nick, I never wanted you to be a star. This school has a championship team and an award-winning coach. I never expected you to start every game."

"Every game, how about *any* game?"

"Don't be a quitter."

"I wouldn't be quitting if you hadn't forced me to join."

"It was a way to meet people."

"Well, I met plenty."

"Don't be fresh. Brett will be terribly disappointed. Your father was going to come for a game, too."

Nick hunkered into the seat. "I'm not Brett, I'm Nick. Wasn't there ever anything Brett tried but didn't do well in? Didn't he ever want to quit something?"

"We're not talking about Brett."

"For once."

"Nick, what is it?"

"Look, Mom, Dad hasn't shown up yet, has he? He'd be mad, anyway, if he drove all the way from Hartford and I never got off the bench. It would waste his valuable time. And it's wasting my valuable time. There's better things for me to do."

They drove in silence until they reached the common. Unconsciously, Julia looked at the fire station. Across the grassy park, Ryan's four-wheel-drive vehicle was in his driveway.

"Did Ryan Branigan tell you to quit?"

"No."

"Then what better things did you have in mind to replace soccer?"

"It was Sean who said I was doing the right thing."

"Sean Branigan? This has nothing to do with any of them. I knew you shouldn't have taken that job."

"They can use me after school this week and it's good exercise besides good money. He showed me the Taft bogs, which won't be ready for a while. There's construction work to do out there, too. I can work for weeks and I'd rather be out there, any day. I really like working with them. I'm learning stuff and it's not a damned waste of time."

"Don't swear."

"Then let me quit."

"I don't want you working on school days. This whole thing was a bad idea. Listen to reason. The soccer season's half over. Stick it out. Don't be a quitter."

"You mean a loser."

"Don't put words in my mouth."

"Mr. Branigan said—"

"Stop it! I've heard enough of the Branigans. Taft bogs, construction . . . they know nothing about you and sports. They have nothing to do with this."

"What's with you, Mom? You're blowing everything out of proportion. Once you were out there with me, I could see you loved all this cranberry stuff. Once you found out I took the job, you were practically dragging me over there. Now I can't mention the name? You've been like this all week. What is it with you and the Branigans?"

Eight

Sean was alone. In the years immediately following Anne's death, Saturday nights had been filled with movies, skating and other daughter-centered activities. Gradually, however, the girls gravitated toward the other houses, the cousins, the aunts who filled the void as best they could. They developed social lives of their own. If they weren't up the hill, their sleep-overs and birthday parties, movies with friends, often filled the longest night of the week.

While he'd finished the CPR courses Friday, his brothers had flooded the main bogs and planned to harvest through the weekend. Kate had grabbed her sleeping bag and hooked up with her buddies the minute he'd finished that afternoon. It was nearly ten o'clock. By this time Suzanne, too, would be stretched out on her classmate's family room floor.

His brothers had been there for him, of course, would always be, but they'd all put in a long day and each had his own family now. No one was needed on the bogs tonight. The night was warm, well above freezing, a respite for all of them except Matt, whose pediatric practice gave him hours as erratic as his brothers'.

Sean stood at the window and looked out at the night with Puck panting in anticipation. Loneliness, was that what it was under his ribs, at the back of his throat, deep in his chest? Was it simple physical need that tightened his diaphragm, raced his pulse, heated his blood?

He rubbed his index finger gently against his lower lip. A week had passed and his body still stirred at the memory of Julia Hollins's transformation under his touch. Was she in too much of his life or not enough? *The luxury of self-indulgence.* He hadn't called her. She hadn't called him.

Puck whined. Sean ruffled his ears. "Okay, boy. It's just you and me tonight." He walked the back lawn to the edge of the pond and let Puck sniff and trot his way over to the sand pile. However, the dog picked up a scent and began digging frantically in the sand. Sean reprimanded him, yanked him out by the collar and swore as he brushed granules from the butterscotch-colored coat. Dogs and kids and solitary walks. Why the hell wasn't it still enough?

When they returned to the house, Puck settled back on his rug, but Sean's restlessness hadn't abated. He grabbed a handful of pretzels and his car keys and headed for the driveway.

The headlights of his four-wheel-drive vehicle bathed the rutted driveway as he bounced along the

cart path toward the company barn. He slowed to a
crawl at the mauled sand pile, which had shifted.
Lights were out at Kevin's; Drew and Holly's were on.

He drove up the hill, past both, and out through the
heavily wooded entrance to the Branigan property.
The car nearly steered itself to the Duxbury Road and
the gates to the Millbrook Country Club. The third set
of Branigan bogs bordered the golf course, and again
Sean turned off the road and followed the hard-
packed path along the dike to the pump house. Twenty
feet from it a blur of scattering bodies tore through his
headlights and back into moonlight. Sean hit the brake
and caught his breath as his heart hammered.

He pulled his flashlight from the glove compart-
ment and aimed it. The single beam of light sliced the
darkness. Sean looked at the dirt, the pump house wall
and the edge of the bog. Half a dozen beer cans lay in
the vines with an unopened six-pack on its side. Another can gurgled as it emptied into his cranberries.

Ahead of him, in the patch of woods between the
course and the bogs, a car engine strained as tires
spun. Damn, but he should have brought Puck, all
bark and no bite. Just the retriever for flushing out a
gaggle of drunk teenagers.

He snapped off the light, let his eyes adjust to the
dark and walked the familiar path. The air smelled of
burning rubber. The engine strained and whined.

"Damn it," he muttered as he recognized the car.
His heart fell. Sean slid his thumb back to the latch of
the flashlight and rapped twice on the driver's window. The glass slid down and Sean blinded the teenager with his beam.

"Turn off the engine."

The car died.

"Aw, hell," came from the passenger's side.

"Shut up, Jason," came from the driver.

"Your mother know where you are?" Sean said.

Somebody snickered in the back seat, then squinted under Sean's beam and blushed.

The boy called Jason leaned over. "Come on, Nick, apologize and let's get out of here." He peered up at Sean. "My friend's new in Millbrook. We were trying to find the country club and took a wrong turn, that's all. We'll get out and push."

"You'll get out, collect every last beer can and get in my Jeep. I want everybody's name and everybody's address."

"Who's he think he is?"

"I'm Lieutenant Branigan," Sean replied.

"Oh, God, a cop. They're so tight with the school, this'll get you kicked off the team, Hollins."

"He's a fire fighter, not a cop. Worse, though, he owns the bogs," Nick muttered.

"Shit, he's a Branigan?"

Nick elbowed his friend. "Just shut up. Yes, he's a Branigan."

Sean slid his hand in the window and opened his palm at the teenager's chest. With a *plunk* Nick dropped the car keys into it.

"Are you going to turn me in to Coach Morris?" Nick Hollins hugged the banister of his staircase. Julia Hollins hugged the throat of her bathrobe and leaned against the horsehair plaster wall trying to slow her heartbeat.

"No," Sean said.

"I guess this means I'm fired."

"Wrong again. I guess this means you'll work your butt off."

"But I screwed up."

"Hasn't affected me yet. You don't show up to-morrow, that's a screwup. We've got a crop that needs harvesting. You've been hired to help. You're part of that team, too, Nick. It's nearly midnight and I'm not about to call all over town looking for a second string replacement. Get to bed and sleep it off. I expect to see you at the barn at 7:00 a.m. whether you feel like it or not."

He turned to Julia. "We need to get your car back here. I'll drive you out."

"Let me throw on something more appropriate." Her eyes glowed with anger and the surprise had dissipated into despair. Her hair was loose, freshly washed and dried, tucked behind one ear. She felt as she had in the orchard—confused and painfully vulnerable.

Sean told her he'd wait in the Jeep. As he opened the front door, Nick called to him from the staircase.

"Mr. Branigan?"

"Yes?"

"Thanks."

"We'll talk."

"I was afraid you'd say that."

"Another time." He pointed to the second floor and left the house.

Julia forced Nick up the stairs in front of her. At his bedroom door he began to apologize. "I'm not drunk, Mom."

"That's little consolation. Go to bed. I don't want to keep Sean waiting. He's angry enough as it is. We have quite a few things to talk about in the morning."

"Look, I'm sorry. All right? I'm not perfect. I screwed up."

"In a very public way. Go to bed. We'll talk in the morning. I need to calm down first and you need to sleep." Once in her room she zipped herself into her jeans and swore. Her bras, slips and tights were at that moment in the gentle cycle of the washing machine. She yanked on the most oversize sweater she owned, a red cotton crewneck, and pressed her hand to her chest to keep her breasts still as she hurried down the stairs.

She began to thank Sean the moment she opened the passenger door and climbed onto the seat, but her voice caught and she fought tears. She pulled hanks of hair from inside her high collar and swiped at her eyes. "I forgot my jacket."

"Buckle up. There's a wool shirt in the back seat, if you need it. The car's warm."

She sniffed as she fumbled in the dark with her seat belt.

"Julia?"

"Never mind. This isn't like me. I can't find the other end for this stupid seat belt."

Sean snapped on the interior car light and yanked the belt into its clip between them. As it stretched against her chest, her breasts strained against the sweater. His glance froze. As he looked up at her, their eyes met.

"I was in a hurry," she whispered, tears on her cheeks. "This isn't like me," she repeated.

He leaned on the steering wheel before finally turning to her. "Isn't like you to forgo your underwear, forget your jacket or dissolve into tears when Nick gives you a run for your money?"

"How can you joke? This sweater's big. I didn't think you'd notice."

"There's been damn little I haven't noticed."

"I didn't want to make you wait. I didn't—" Her voice broke again. She stared at the ceiling and blinked hard. "I'm completely humiliated. It isn't like Nick. I don't know what got into him, what you must think of him."

"I think of him as a sixteen-year-old, stretching every boundary he's got. That's what you do at sixteen. Frankly, Dr. Hollins, this is a pleasant surprise. I like you much better flustered and humiliated. It gives me the advantage, for once." He snapped off the light and turned on the ignition as he eased the Jeep out of her driveway.

Julia cringed. There was nothing inside her but the steady rhythm of her still-pounding pulse. They rumbled through the village while she tried to think of something to say. "Sean, I never meant for you to— This is completely unexpected."

He laughed. "How nice to have you on the defensive."

"I think we should talk."

"Nick's all right. Your expectations might be a little high. He seems to think so, anyway. Brett casts a big shadow, I gather."

"I mean about other things."

"Too personal?"

"I'd like to keep Nick out of this."

"He's a Branigan employee. I'm flattered that he's felt comfortable enough with me to let off some steam."

"Nevertheless, that makes other things ridiculously complicated."

"What other things? Us? The orchard?"

"Yes." She leaned back against the headrest. They passed the fire station, Ryan and Sky's darkened house. The village gave way to a development.

"I'm listening."

She waited until they were on the county road. "It's been a long week."

"No phone calls to break it up."

"I thought you might. Call me, that is."

"I thought I might, too, but damned if I knew what I'd say."

"Because of my reaction in the orchard?"

"No, mine."

This wasn't going as she'd hoped. Nothing in her life was going as she'd hoped. Emotion closed her throat and still made her breath catch. She swiped angrily at a stray tear and sat up. "Since I didn't hear from you all week, I thought you might have changed your mind and still presumed that I was using Kate to get to you. You're right about how it looks. I came out to the bogs with Nick last Friday night, and then showed up the next morning. And then in the orchard... I think I've given you the wrong impression."

They stopped at an intersection and Julia listened to the click of the signal indicator. He turned right.

"Sean?"

"I'm thinking about those impressions and which ones were wrong."

"It's not like you to tease."

"Who's teasing? Our lives are interlocking like puzzle pieces. You pounce on Kate and I jump into your life. I jump into your life and there's Nick in mine. That would be enough for anybody regardless of the rest of it.''

"It's the rest of it I'm trying to talk about."

"You mean the pass I made at you in the orchard?"

"Yes."

"And now you're in my car in next to nothing."

"If you think this is next to nothing, I'd better crawl into the back for that shirt, now." She ran her hand through her hair until it was pulled back off her face.

From the moment Sean had stepped into her house, his demeanor had changed, softened. The edge was gone from his voice, replaced with a disconcerting sincerity just short of sensual. She could swear he was enjoying the chaos.

"I was kidding," he said.

"How rare. I wasn't aware that Sean had a sense of humor. Are you sure you're not Drew?"

"After midnight, on the way to our bogs, Drew Branigan had better not be joking about your unbridled breasts."

"Goodness."

"Won't do my adrenaline system any good, either."

"You're certainly different tonight. You're making jokes—at my expense—but still jokes. I see so much of you in Drew. The physical resemblance, of course, but even that first afternoon when I mistook him for you, I thought it was as if your twin is what you could be, what you might have been, before you lost your wife or before Kate hit puberty. Before you took on the world."

"You sure as hell cut right to the chase."

"Trying to understand people is my profession."

A stand of birch gleamed briefly in the headlights. "I hate that you can look at Kate and see with absolute clarity what I should do to make things better, what I'm doing wrong, my failings as a father."

"I've never said you were failing."

"You didn't have to, Julia. If I weren't, we'd never have met."

Sean skirted a pothole and passed the Millbrook Medical Clinic. Only an occasional car disturbed the dark sweep of open land.

"Bring Kate and Suzanne home."

"I thought we were talking about the orchard."

"This is safer."

"This little drive all the way back out here isn't about *my* kids. If we're going into sociological discussions, let's talk over your son's behavior tonight."

"Sean Branigan, you have the most irritating habit of shutting yourself up like a clam the minute I get too close, or the subject gets too personal. Despite everything else that's clouding this, you and I do have a professional relationship for one fourteen-year-old reason. You can't confess that you feel like a failure as a father, then refuse to discuss it."

"I just did."

"We met for professional reasons and we can lay those to rest if you'll just stop being so afraid of a little outside influence."

"Outside interference."

"Call it what you want. You're not failing as a father or as anything else. Kate doesn't need my counseling, in fact you'll be getting a note in the mail from me asking for another conference to tell you just that."

"We've had our conference."

"All I'm asking for is a chance to talk with you. Kate's finished her detention, and her name's gone to the high school to be matched with a tutor. Once she starts achieving in class, and gets a sense of boundaries at home, she should feel much better. I hope it's occurred to you that when she feels better, you will, too."

"That is your expertise, isn't it—how people feel."

"How they feel makes a great deal of difference in how they act."

Empathy softened, warmed, somehow shaped her words. His defenses were close to disintegrating. Fear of Julia Hollins might have been the buffer he needed, but what this woman did to his body, not to mention his temperament, had nothing to do with fright. He threw up the strongest smoke screen he could think of.

"If you're the expert on feelings, you might start with those closest to you. Branigans aren't the only ones in need of some attention."

"I was wondering how long it would take for you to throw this back in my face. I admit Nick's having adjustment problems. New kid on the block and all that. After tonight I can imagine what you must think of him. I would have fired him on the spot."

"I'm not throwing anything in your face and he doesn't need any more rejection."

"He doesn't need to get away with illegal, self-centered behavior."

"He's a good kid going through rough times. Doesn't that ring a bell with you? New town, no big brother, mother breathing down his neck. Absent father."

"Sean, this really isn't appropriate."

"Because the topic's a Hollins not a Branigan?"

"Yes, maybe."

Julia stayed quiet as he swung the Jeep onto the dirt. How much like Drew had he been? Had his sense of humor evaporated? He pulled up next to her car. "Then let's get back to the orchard discussion. I nearly kissed you in those apple trees last Saturday and I haven't thought about much since. My life's becoming an open book. I'm asking for a page out of yours. Forget Nick. Give me a status report on your husband."

"Nick's father and I've been divorced for five years. Paul's in Hartford mostly, Nantucket in the summer, Vail at Christmas."

"Fast lane. Hard to compete?"

"I have no desire to compete with Paul's life-style."

"Has he remarried?"

"He's never without company, but Paul's not one for monogamy. He's reliving his own adolescence. His idea of being a parent is throwing money at his children and playing buddy when they're with him. There's no doubt that if I called him about tonight he'd side with Nick. Boys will be boys, and all that."

"The rites of passage."

"Don't tell me you agree?"

"I've been there, that's all, with no parents, remember? Nick's finding his way and feeling the pressure."

The car smelled faintly of Julia's shampoo, a fresh and clean scent that had filled his head the moment she'd closed the door, one that would linger this night as it had that first morning in her office. Her hair, shiny and loose for the first time, was nearly luminescent in the reflected light.

He forced himself to concentrate. "The boys were stuck over by those pines. We pushed out the car before we left. There's no damage."

"The damage doesn't have to be physical. How am I going to be able to trust him when he's out with his friends?"

"An episode of bad judgment doesn't destroy anything, Julia. Don't most of us learn from them?"

"I've always talked to him about underage drinking. He knows better than to drink and drive."

"He knows you won't tolerate it and now he knows I won't, either. I drove every one of his friends home, too, lecturing all the way."

"Would you turn him in to his coach?"

"Hasn't it occurred to you that that's what he wants? Sneaking beers in semipublic places is a way to get him kicked off the soccer team. Leaving the team has been a battle between the two of you and this settles it by a third party. He breaks the rules in public, he gets canned. You have no say in it."

"Which makes me helpless."

"The way he's been feeling."

"Are you sure you're not a psychologist?"

"I know a frustrated teenager when I see one. I'm the father of one, remember? Nick's trying to make his way, trying to make friends. My God, it could have been much worse. There may be worse to come. Puberty—he's reinventing himself, or at least that's what you'd tell me."

She jangled her car keys. "Should I let him quit?"

Sean smiled and put up his hand. "Oh no, you don't. I bow out on that question. Just take his opinion seriously."

"Yes, Doc. There were no girls in the car?"

"Just the guys."

"I suppose I should be thankful. There hasn't been anybody special yet, except a few crushes. Now, being new in Millbrook, he's starting all over again. I worry about Brett, too, dorm life for the first time, few restrictions. These are dangerous times."

"Does Paul talk to them?"

"About sexual responsibility? Emotional commitment? He's the antithesis of everything I try to teach them." She pressed her fist to the bridge of her nose and bit her lip. "Forgive me."

Sean touched her shoulder, then her hair and the warmth coursed straight down his spine. "Do you still love Paul?"

She shook her head. "Don't misunderstand. It's parenthood that has me all unstrung tonight, that's all."

She stared through the dark windshield. Her breathing was rapid and her breasts strained against her sweater, still held fast by her seat belt. Her fragrance, the sweep of her hair, even her breathing stimulated long-dormant sensations in him. He should make another joke, break the tension, lighten the atmosphere with a compliment. Instead, he sat and savored the gooseflesh, heat, the steady thud of his pounding heart. He felt as he had in the orchard—alive.

Julia turned as Sean yanked the door handle. He got out and drew a breath as if he'd been drowning. He went to the front of the Jeep and leaned against the hood, arms across his sweatered chest. Julia put on his wool shirt and followed.

"Is this a better place to talk?"

"Safer."

"You're confusing me."

"That seems to be the emotion of the moment. Do you have the kind of support I do, family, some uncles hanging around somewhere for your boys?"

"No one close enough for a weekend visit. That's why I talked Nick into the Police League program. The counselor at the high school suggested it."

"Counselors see counselors?"

"I get advice where I can, even from cranberry growers, I guess." She cleared her throat. "I think it's time for me to get up off the couch, Doc. It's your turn and I'll strike a deal, seeing as you're in such a mellow mood."

"Mellow?"

"Compared to the Sean Branigan I've dealt with so far. You don't have to come into school if I can have that conference with you tonight. You were in a fine mood a minute ago, albeit at my expense. I know it's late, but could you come back to my house one more time? We'll talk. Cooperate and I'll promise to leave you alone."

"Somehow I doubt that. Hell of it is, I'm not sure I want you to." He looked at the stars. "Out here'll do fine. You've wormed your way into our lives, Julia. I'll hear what you have to say out here on my bogs, where I still have some control over my life." He grinned. It felt good. "Shoot. You have my undivided attention."

"Now? Here? This isn't what I had in mind."

"Nick and his buddies over there at my pump house and you in my car tonight weren't on my agenda, either. Part of that wasn't completely unpleasant. I'm in a decent mood and on familiar territory. I'll listen here. It's warm enough. Take it or leave it."

"Do I have a choice?"

"No."

"You strike a hard bargain. I guess I'll take it."

"Then get comfortable and talk to me."

Julia wasn't comfortable, hadn't been since Sean delivered Nick to the house. It was a discomfort charged with emotion, innuendo and possibility. Part of her wanted the familiarity of her living room, the security of her son one floor above. The other part of her, however, wanted the bogs and the moonlight and Sean Branigan half shadowed as he was. She yanked the jacket tighter.

"The main point I want to make is that you're a wonderful man, a good father. You have to trust your instincts. Your daughters need one household—yours. Holly and Erin and the others are fine for filling in, but Sean, they need their father full-time."

"I hate this."

She waited, long enough to hear the distant whistle of a train. She brushed his cheek, lightly, as he had her hair. "I know."

He pushed her hand away gently. "Don't get all womanly and psychological on me. I'm confused enough. Hell, most of the time I don't have a clue how to be what Kate and Suzy need. Anne was always there for them. It seems like half their lives I was on all-night shifts at the fire station."

"Concentrate on what you have to offer. Your daughters need a steady, constant source of love and authority—that was always you, and now it's more important than ever. They've adjusted to life without their mother. In many ways you've forced them to adjust to life without their father, as well."

"That was never the intention, never!"

"These are critical years. We won't resolve any-thing tonight, but think about it. As I said before, I have far more pressing problems than Kate. She's wonderful. She'll be fine with support and encour-agement. Give her boundaries. Give her your time."

"Time. You make it sound so damn easy."

"You've had proof tonight that it's not, but love and determination can move mountains. That's all I had to say. Just promise me you'll think it over. And please don't forget that I'll always listen if you ever want to talk to someone outside your family. Kate knows that. You should, too."

"Love and determination. What about schedules and mortgages and giving them the rest of what they need like food on the table and college tuition?"

"Follow your heart, Sean."

He shoved his hands into his pockets and walked toward her car. She caught up and stood in front of him until she was able to look up into his shadowed face. She put her hands on his shoulders.

She'd had romance; she'd had marriage. She was fine without the heartache of either. Yet this man, shouldering nearly more than he could bare, touched her as no one else ever had. A Sean Branigan she didn't know, hadn't known existed, had emerged and she was too drawn to him to follow anything related to sound judgment.

He took his hands from his pockets and played with her hair. He pressed her temples as if he could feel the throbbing under his palms. Once again he ran his finger over her bottom lip. The sensation was nearly unbearable. Denial, sublimation—there were half a dozen ten-dollar words for it—were useless.

This time he kissed her. His lips were warm, soft, as
he brushed back and forth over hers. She held his
shoulders and played against his tongue, intoxicated
by the sensation. Sean Branigan made her acutely
aware that she was a woman, one who momentarily
would have to make a decision.

Moonlight and woods, private property. The moment he'd insisted on talking here rather than her
house, she'd understood. Acres of secluded glens,
children "up the hill" living nearly separate lives...
How cleanly this man separated the needs in his life.
His daughters had strong mother figures in their lives.
Five intact families supplied his emotional support.
After a long, happy marriage she couldn't fault him
for seeking only physical gratification. How often
since Anne? How careful?

Her thoughts blurred in a rush of pleasure it was
getting difficult to conceal. His mouth was soft, pli-
ant, sensuous. She felt his hands over her shoulders
and down her back, but it was her breasts that ached
and her heart that pounded. He moaned softly as she
hugged him.

For a moment they were still. She put her cheek
against his chest and listened to the steady rhythm. He
kissed her hair and caught his breath.

"I suppose these bogs are full of romantic inter-
ludes," Julia finally said into his sweater.

"A few." He was no good at the repartee, casual
episodes, or spontaneous sex that no one ever seemed
to regret or think twice about. During a long, happy
marriage, all that had passed him by. More to the
point, as spontaneous as this was, there wasn't anything casual about it. This woman was far too entan-
gled in his life already. Who knew what she expected,

what she was used to. Adult desire in a complicated world—he was no better at this than he was at heading his own household.

His arms were around her. They stood together. They breathed together. Did she know how it aroused him to feel the weight of her breasts against his chest? Could she guess at the erotic images coursing through his head? Hadn't she been embarrassed in the Jeep not fifteen minutes earlier? Did she mean this as a simple hug?

She loosened herself and looked up at him. "At the Bittersweet Bogs picnic, Sky started to tell me about some bogs by the golf course. She was interrupted and said I should ask you about them. Would that be the story you thought inappropriate for a school counselor, that Friday night?"

"It might."

"If Sky's story is funny, I'd like to hear it. Before I go, I'd like to share something light with you, that has nothing to do with teenagers."

"Sorry, it has everything to do with teenagers, puberty, too. Theirs anyway."

"Tell me. We're not responsible for them."

"I was then. That's half the reason I married so young, to get away from the responsibility." Sean shoved his hands back into his pockets. "Never mind. I'm off the subject. This is one for a psychologist, Dr. Hollins."

"You've come to the right place."

"Ryan had a landscaping job at the Millbrook Country Club the summer he graduated from high school. The Schuylers arrived for the summer. There was Sky on the courts, at the pool, as stunning as she is now, rich, spoiled, half a dozen Ivy Leaguers on the string.''

"In theory, beyond his reach," Julia said.

"Completely. Still there he was, day after day."

"One of those wild Branigan boys from out on the bogs. Forbidden fruit."

"Rich girl, struggling, orphaned boy, raging hormones, nothing in common. The two of them spent that torrid teenage summer together, despite her parents, despite all the chaperoning Kevin, Drew and I did. To separate them, Sky's parents shipped her off to Europe but the night before she left, over in those pines...the earth moved, bells rang, who knows what else." The flush crept up from under his sweater.

Damn his heart! It was thundering as if he were sharing something far more intimate than a silly story about his brother. He smiled sardonically. "She went off to Vienna, then college. Her father died soon after. Her mother rented out the house and kept the family in Palm Beach and Boston. Thirteen years later, Sky waltzed back into town and rekindled a fire the likes of which even my profession couldn't douse."

"Is there a punch line?"

"I'm not sure I should have brought this up, after all."

"Finish the story and I'll let you know."

He took a breath and let it out slowly. "After they married, they weren't having much luck conceiving, so they came back out here to where it all began. Rekindled the magic, fertile magic this time. Hayley was born nine months later, then Sophie came along last July."

Julia counted on her fingers. "She was conceived on a night like last Saturday, while they monitored for frost."

"Yes, last October."

"Painfully romantic. I hope you and your wife had moments like those."

Sean watched the bogs and tried to make sense of the night. "It was different with Anne," he murmured. "She was a wonderful mother and wife. We had a strong, happy marriage. Things were different for me, that's all. We were childhood sweethearts. Anne was all I ever knew, all I ever wanted. Marrying her had a lot to do with having lost my parents. It was all tied up in getting away from the responsibility Kevin was saddled with. Anne and I were never secret lovers out on the bogs."

"Not even once?"

"We had a bedroom." He smiled at her. "You'd think my settling down would be a good example for my brothers, but they held out for years, even my twin. I never had to work at romance the way Drew did or fight it like Kevin and Jody."

"More stories?"

"You've heard enough about the Branigans."

He looked at the shadows draping her shoulders. Julia Hollins had managed to open that place deep inside against his heart, the place kept safe for so long. The loneliness that had brought him out here hours earlier had lost its edge, the hollowness no longer yawned. She listened. She understood. She knew. Despite every effort, from anger to humor, the shock was the emotional relief. The result was pleasure. Both intensified every time he was with her. Desire kept his heart pounding. When he brushed her hair off her shoulders, she put her arms around his neck.

He whispered at her temple. "I don't know if it's the night, or the circumstances or a combination of both, but you're a different person. Your hair's down and so are your defenses. I'm the one in need of chaperoning on these bogs."

She opened her hands against his chest and tilted her head. Her kiss was hesitant, chaste, but sure. He returned it and shifted back and forth as he had against her mouth, but now against her sweater. He let the fabric of his shirt tease her and he moaned softly as she arched her back. Pleasure began as warmth, then a bone-deep ache that burned its way to desire.

"Sean," she panted. "Please remember that underneath I'm not wearing—"

"Your unbridled breasts are magnificent."

She looked at him wide-eyed, then grinned. "You're the one who's different tonight, you and your sense of humor."

He held her and rocked softly, methodically, shirt against sweater, until she was molded against him again. It was not a simple hug. She kissed him, deeply this time, passionately. Slowly he opened the Branigan shirt she wore. He cupped her breasts, with his fingers, palms, thumbs against dream-soft flesh. Her kisses deepened and he massaged small circles in the fabric, stunned at the pleasure coursing through him. Denial and self-control, integral parts of this desire, sharpened his senses, pricked his conscience. Introspection edged the heat.

"I know what you must be used to out here," she managed.

"You're as ripe as the berries."

"Where's the frost when I need it?" Julia whispered.

Sean closed his eyes. School, his daughters, her son, her profession, he called every one of them to mind while he still had the sense. "The voice of reason?"

She was panting against his palms, wide-eyed, but she nodded and he slowly closed the shirt and buttoned it, neck to hem. He raised his face to the crisp October night. Not now, not after all this time. Not her.

Sean shoved his hand through his hair and shone the flashlight on her car. "Time to call it a night on all counts. Time to get headed in the proper direction."

"I had a few more questions. I wanted you to keep..." She couldn't seem to catch her breath. "Talking."

God, how his heart hammered. "I know it was my idea to talk out here, but there's nothing left. Or too much," he whispered. "I'm still willing to listen." He paused. "Do you understand that I can't hold you and spill my guts, not even silly Branigan stories—not without—" He fingered her hair. "To put it delicately, physically I'm at the point of no return, Julia."

"I didn't mean for it to go that far."

"Who knows what either of us meant." He shone the flashlight on her. "If I'd asked just now, would you have said yes?"

She put her fingers against his mouth. "If I'd asked, would you?" She smiled at his expression.

When she opened her own car door, she turned briefly. "I think we need some distance from this. Next week—I'd appreciate it if you wouldn't call. Not that you have."

"And I don't expect to hear from you."

"You won't."

"So, am I grounded for life?"

"Would it help?" Julia was back in her bathrobe at six forty-five the following morning. She passed a glass of juice to Nick as he pulled on his jacket.

"Psycho-babble. You always answer a question with a question." When she smiled, he grumbled, "Don't turn it into a joke."

"Nick, I was smiling because Mr. Branigan had the same reaction."

"Which Mr. Branigan?"

"Sean, actually."

"You trying to psyche him out, too?"

"No, of course not." She could feel a flush rise from her diaphragm. Her breasts tingled, intensified by the memory of Sean's hands, his thumbs. Goose-flesh contracted her skin. She turned to the coffee-pot. "To answer your question, no, I don't think grounding is the issue. Putting you in the hands of the Branigans will do more good than sentencing you to your room."

"Boy, that's a switch. Last I remember you lectured the heck out of me about the Branigans not having anything to say about my life." He narrowed his gaze. "What'd you two talk about out there on the bogs? You were gone a long time."

"Plenty."

"Me, probably."

"A logical guess."

"Don't go dissecting my life."

"Don't give me reason to. Eat your cereal and tell me why you did something so blatantly foolish and risky last night."

"That means you talked about me."

"You were the reason for my being out there, Nick."

He sighed. "I don't know why I did it. I didn't sneak and scheme behind your back if that's what you're worried about. The guys had the beer and I knew the place."

"How many of them are on varsity teams at school?"

"What are you getting at?"

"You and soccer come to mind."

Nick drained his juice and avoided her glance. "If this is the third degree, I think I'd rather be grounded."

"I think you'd rather be off the soccer team."

"That, too."

"You've lost the use of the car without specific permission. And don't even think about buying one."

"What about soccer?"

"Letting you quit now becomes a reward for your irresponsible behavior."

"Jeez! Why do you have to be a psychologist?"

"I'm a concerned parent, darling. You don't need a degree in psychology for that." She peered out the window. "Ryan's here. Don't make him wait."

Nick grabbed his waders. "Do you think he knows?"

"If he does, he's been told for your own good."

"Right. He used to be a cop. He'll have every squad car in Millbrook on my butt."

"With my blessing." She opened the door and tried to hug him, but he scooted sideways and out to the waiting truck.

Once back in her bedroom, Julia stripped for a shower. Blatantly risky and foolish behavior. She was as guilty of it as her son. She yanked on the faucet and pulled comfortable clothes from her closet, underwear from her dresser. Neatly stacked lingerie lined her drawers. Unable to sleep after she'd driven herself home from the bogs, she'd dried and folded and put away the load of wash at one in the morning, wishing the entire time that she'd followed Sean to his Jeep in a corset, girdle and ski parka. Now she picked up a bra and pressed her breastbone against the second flush of the day.

What if he *had* asked, the cranberry grower, the fire fighter who couldn't keep his own house in order? She'd behaved as though she were the besotted teenager he'd described. Of course he'd expected her to continue. They were consenting adults, enjoying the moment without complications or expectations.

In the five years since her divorce she'd never been able to pull that off, least of all last night. She was no more appropriate for Sean Branigan than Sky had been for Ryan. Yet she wasn't Sky, a woman without a care. She was a mother, a role model for two teenagers. She was also ashamed of herself.

The mirrored wall over the sink was beginning to fog, but Julia paused as she pulled back the shower curtain. She touched her hair; he liked it down. She pivoted. Her breasts were ample, still firm. *Magnificent,* he'd said. She didn't smile.

How many since Anne? How often? Could he guess how long it had been since she'd felt like a woman?

Did he have any idea that his touch would ignite possibilities she'd spend the rest of the weekend grappling with? She got in the tub and raised her face. Tears mixed with the spray.

Nine

Wednesday evening Kate Branigan was still complaining as she turned from her bedroom closet. "I don't know why I have to stay here, all my stuff's at Aunt Holly's. I don't even have the shirt I want for school tomorrow."

"Because this is your room, your house, your family." Sean, in his usual neutral spot just outside Kate's door frame, had barely enough energy left to keep from becoming embroiled in another confrontation. Instead he forced a smile and focused on the teddy-bear border framing her windows.

Kate grimaced. "You never used to think so. Besides, it's only you, Dad, not a family."

"You, Suzy and I make a family. This is who we are, Katie. Try and pretend that's acceptable." Sean swallowed the hurt. "I'm sorry. That was sarcastic and I didn't mean it. You exhaust me, darling."

"Yeah, well, then let me go back up the hill."

"After the harvest when I'm back at the fire station, you'll be up there, plenty. When I'm home, I want to go over your school assignments. Let me review with you for tests. I'm supposed to, you know."

"Dr. Hollins's big idea?"

"She wants you to succeed."

"Yuk."

"Have you seen any more of her?"

"Nah. I finished my detention and she says as long as I do my work, things'll stay fine. She's okay. She's pretty good at knowing what you mean, even when you can't put the right words together. I guess I don't mind her as long as I don't get yanked into her office for stuff."

"That's up to you."

"I know, I know. She says she has to look over my grades for a while."

"Make her proud."

"That's exactly what she said I should do about you."

"It's what parents live for."

"Yuk."

"You know she's there if you ever want to talk about other stuff, too. Girl stuff, boy trouble, grades."

"I know. We have talked some. She sort of gets into my head and figures things out with me."

"Good."

"Now can I go up the hill?"

"You're stuck here, kiddo. Uncle Jody's in New York on business and I invited Aunt Megan and her boys for dinner. She's on her way with her best garlic bread. That should help."

"I'd rather eat at her house."

"Sorry. It's spaghetti right here, homework right here, bedtime right here." He was careful not to step over the threshold to her room. "Suzy's setting the table. Come and help me make the salad."

"And baby-sit Evan and Flynn when Aunt Megan gets here."

"Weren't you just talking about more family?"

Sean went back down to the kitchen determined to salvage the evening. Julia Hollins, compassionate giver of advice to harried parents, was the one he should have harangued. Three days into full-fledged fatherhood, his daughters had done little but complain, sulk or trade stories of misery in endless phone conversations with their friends.

He hadn't called Julia, however, hadn't spoken with her since *the incident at the bogs,* as he'd come to think of it. He tried not to think of it. The reminiscing about Ryan must have gone to his head—or parts he'd refused to think about since. Until he could make sense of his response to Julia Hollins, physically and emotionally, he had no intention of coming within shouting distance. For the present, full-time fatherhood took what felt like every ounce of energy he possessed.

His sister-in-law was a far safer choice for an evening buffer between himself and his daughters. Megan had laughed and called it an act of desperation. There was more to it, however. She and her sisters had lost their own mother as teenagers. It was a bond the O'Connor women shared with the Branigan men they'd married, and a balm to Kate and Suzanne. Erin, Megan, Bridget, any one of them knew as much about what Kate and Suzanne were feeling as Julia Hollins. Since the weekend, however, Sean's biggest problem was not his daughters' emotional situation, it was his. His emotions, his behavior. He was becoming obsessed with self-analysis and it hadn't done a damn bit of good.

As he came down the stairs, Suzanne came through the back door carrying her nine-month-old cousin Flynn into the family room. She had two-year-old Evan by the hand. Sean went out and caught Megan at the driveway.

"Thanks for coming."

The fiery redhead kissed his cheek. "You sounded desperate. I'm a sucker for the old motherless household line every time. Besides, Jody and I are getting serious about house hunting. I want to talk to you about your contractor. We've always loved this design."

"Contractor?"

She smiled at his anguish. "Are you listening?"

"Sorry. I was thinking about my latest heart-to-heart with Kate."

"Your girls will be fine. Kate's turning into a woman, Sean. Half her discontent is growing pains, too many freckles, nose is wrong, feet too big, bosoms too small." She patted his arm. "Imagine what my dad went through with three of us feeling that way."

"Hugh O'Connor deserves sainthood."

"So he tells us. It was my red hair I couldn't stand; Kate grumbles about hers. I can sure help in that category."

"You sound like the adjustment counselor."

Megan raised an eyebrow. "That would be Julia Hollins. Quite a looker, from what I could tell at the bogs two weeks ago."

"She was curious about the harvest."

"Weren't we all at one point or another?" Megan hugged him. "You Branigans and your blushes. Melts a girl's heart, every time."

"Yours took longer than most."

"Your levelheaded brother and I were both in the midst of career crises when we met. Talk to Jody if you need some pointers. He was quite . . . persuasive in his courting days."

"I'm not courting."

"Heart-melting on your agenda?"

"No."

"Would you tell me if it were?"

"No again."

She laughed and hugged him. Sean grumbled, but returned the embrace as a familiar sedan pulled into the driveway. Nick Hollins got out and pulled waders and a manila mailing envelope from the trunk.

"Mr. Branigan, the other Mr. Branigan—Drew—asked me to drop these off on my way home. He said this is the information from the Wisconsin Growers Association you were looking for. I was getting my paycheck from Mrs. Branigan and I think I left my sweatshirt at this bog. The other Mr. Branigan—Ryan—said it might be in the pump house."

Sean laughed. "It would probably be a lot easier to call us by our first names." He took his arm from around Megan. "Have you met this Mrs. Branigan?"

The teenager shook her hand. "At the bogs that Saturday, I think. There were an awful lot of you."

"Then call me Megan, if it'll make things easier. If you'll excuse me, I'm going to get dinner started. Sean, I think it's time Kate and I visited the beauty parlor together. I have an appointment at my old

Newbury Street salon tomorrow. We could both use a day in Boston. Suzy, too." She waved at them and headed for the kitchen.

Nick carried the waders to the garage. As Megan went into the house, he looked at Sean. "I guess I still owe you an apology for last Saturday night."

"You worked your butt off Sunday. I think we're square."

"My mom doesn't think so, but thanks."

Sean walked with him across the back lawn toward the pump house. "What did you decide about the soccer team?"

The boy shrugged. "The season's nearly over. I guess I can tough it out."

"Whose decision?"

"Mine."

"Your mother must be pleased."

Nick gave him a studied look. "I guess I owe her, too."

"How about sticking with it for both of you?"

As they skirted the pond, Nick tossed a stone and watched the ripples. "Do you ever feel like everything you do is for somebody else?"

"Some would say that's the purpose of life. Try to get some satisfaction out of it, yourself. Makes life sweeter."

"Yeah, maybe. Coach Morris says I'm starting in the game tomorrow night."

"There you go! Kate's been nagging me all week to take her. We'll bring a Branigan cheering section."

"Thanks. Kate talks about soccer a lot at the bogs. She plays for the middle school?"

"Loves the sport."

"We're playing Bayside. They stink so the coach is giving second string a chance. My dad's coming so at least I won't be wasting his time. Last time I never got off the bench. Boy was he mad."

"Probably disappointed for you."

"Right."

Sean fished the crumpled sweatshirt from the pump house and they headed back.

"I like this work. Right now it's the only time I get to drive the car."

"Lost privileges?"

"Yeah, well, Mom could have done worse things. Did you talk to her or something?"

"I might have pointed out the fact that I remember what it felt like to be a teenager. I don't think your mother knows what it's like to be a sixteen-year-old boy, Nick."

"I bet some of you guys tore this town up."

"You'll never hear it from me."

The teenager looped his sweatshirt over his shoulder. "Look, I gotta go. Mom's been chewing my head off all week as it is. Something's really bugging her and my old man's call about did her in."

"Divorce can do that."

"It's not the divorce, it's the girlfriends. Dad's latest is from Boston. Danielle has an awesome apartment. I stay with them sometimes. Dad's had a lot of—friends—since he and Mom split. Mom thinks it's a bad influence and I'll turn into a sex fiend and get every disease in the book."

"There's always that chance."

He glanced sideways at Sean. "Were you?"

"A sex fiend? I made it legal early. Married the only girl I ever really got serious about. You take your time, Nick."

"Heck, the only girl I'm interested in barely knows I'm alive. Kelly Baxter drives the hottest car."

"Watch yourself in hot cars."

"Right. I haven't even—you know—done it."

Sean masked his surprise at the teenager's willingness to divulge something so personal. "Good. It's way too soon. There's no rush."

"I know, I know, but things are different now."

"Things are *deadly dangerous* now. My wife and I waited, even though it was a million years ago."

"Not a Branigan."

He slung his arm around the teenager as they reached the car. "I think you've got some wrong impressions about us."

"Most of the impressions are pretty good ones. Mom went from chewing my head off about working for you to thinking you're wonderful for not firing me."

"Canning you would have been our loss. You're a good worker."

"Thanks."

"Tell your mother I said hello. You and I'll talk some more."

"I don't know. I'm kind of sorry already I told you about the sex stuff."

"I consider it privileged information."

"Yeah?"

"Yeah. Kelly going to the game?"

"She said she might."

"One more reason to stay on the team."

"Girls kind of like it, I guess."

"Mine included. I'll see you at the game Friday night."

"I'd like that. I gotta go. It's my night to cook. Mom's gonna have my rear end for being so late. Anyway, Mrs. Branigan's calling you."

"Oregano?" Megan was asking from the door.

Sean signaled, then patted Nick's shoulder. "Come for dinner some night, you and your mom." He was tempted to finish the conversation with a message for Julia. He was following her advice; he was floundering with the girls; fatherhood was draining his confidence faster than a bog with a hole in the dike. Now what did she recommend?

Instead, he waved the boy off with a final encouraging word about his work and the upcoming game. He'd found a kid who listened. Would he be a better father if he'd had sons instead of daughters? Life without his girls was unthinkable, but the female in any form still mystified him. He went to help Megan with the spaghetti, digesting Nick's information as he entered his house.

Ten

"**A**nd he probably didn't mean it, but he wants us to come for dinner sometime."

Julia was listening with half an ear as Nick offered, yet again, another explanation for being late. Because she suspected that he'd skipped soccer practice, he was adamantly defending himself with Branigan anecdotes, explanations of picking up paychecks, and returning waders, not to mention sweatshirts in pump houses.

"Which Mr. Branigan wants to feed us?"

"Sean. It doesn't matter. He was probably just being polite. Mrs. Branigan didn't ask."

"Mrs. Branigan?"

"Megan. Weren't you listening?"

"Since you're late I'm too busy trying to throw dinner together." Too busy trying not to look nonplussed. A man who opens his heart, nearly makes love to her, then negates it all by remaining incommunicado for a week suggests dinner to her son. All right, so they'd agreed not to call each other. But still . . . She caught Nick staring at her and busied herself in the refrigerator. She didn't need this, any of it.

"Mom?"

"Here, peel some carrots."

Thursday after soccer practice Nick arrived home in the passenger seat of a late-model sports car driven by a teenager who tossed a mane of blond hair as she pulled into the driveway. They sat with the engine idling and the next time Julia looked the driver was shaking her head.

"Kelly Baxter" was all the information Nick divulged besides, "Yes, I wore my seat belt." Beyond that he was silent and opted for leaf raking and a late supper, as if he still had energy to be burned.

Julia watched him through the window. What teenage troubles, what demons did he exorcise as he raked? How badly did he want to impress this girl Friday night, or was he pressured by his father's impending attendance. "Don't let us down," he'd said to Nick on the phone the night before.

" 'Don't let us down.' What the heck's that supposed to mean?" Nick had muttered to her as he hung up.

It was no surprise that he enjoyed his work on the bogs. Physical labor, even before the divorce, had always been his solace. "We could all do with a little hard labor," she murmured as she tossed a salad and turned off the soup. Nick's labor had stopped, however, when she opened the door to call him to supper.

The teenager was at the curb talking, not to Kelly, but an in-line skater. Even under the helmet and joint pads, Julia recognized the figure of Kate Branigan. The inherited cheek-to-cheek flush and flashing green eyes were unmistakable. Julia walked to the street and asked for a demonstration.

Kate's flush deepened as she glanced from Julia to her son. "I didn't know this was your house. It's a good street for Rollerblading because it's a dead end. Aunt Sky wants me out of traffic. Branigans are so overprotective. My dad and Uncle Jody are at Uncle Ryan's so they can talk about some legal stuff. Pretty boring. Jeez." She finally sighed like a balloon losing air.

Julia smiled at the furtive glances, painful blushes, stammered explanations and wondered how long the crush on her son had been simmering. In-line skates on a safe dead-end street: a brilliant excuse. Nick seemed oblivious. Men always were.

"Nick says you're a whiz on the eggbeaters these days."

"Thanks."

"Anything ready this weekend?"

"That's up to Nick and my uncles. I'm going into Boston. Some shopping and a haircut on Newbury Street."

"Nick will be in the city, too," Julia replied.

Again Kate's green eyes brightened. She focused on the *Harvard University* and college seal printed on Nick's sweatshirt as if he might make eye contact. "Really? I love Cambridge and Newbury Street. I go into Boston a lot. No one gives a decent haircut in Millbrook. The food's much better, too." She adjusted her knee pads and pushed off.

"No decent haircuts in Millbrook and the food's better?" Nick muttered incredulously.

"Don't spoil it," Julia whispered.

"Spoil what?"

"The moment."

"Give it a rest, Mom. I knew she was going to Boston. The Branigans were talking about it when I stopped by yesterday. She's a kid."

"Probably wishing she were as old as Kelly Baxter."

"What does she have to do with Kelly?" He turned as Kate executed a perfect figure eight. "Whoa, she's good."

"Tell her," Julia replied. "Be a good audience, Nick. When she's finished, come in for supper."

Julia laid out the salad and bread. Who was she to give advice on romance? A divorced psychologist who couldn't keep her own house in order.

Rain threatened Friday night, but she went to the high school soccer game anyway. It would have been far easier not to. Ex-husband and female companion were bundled in their designer outdoor wear smack in the middle of the bleachers.

Nick alternated between shivering on the bench and playing strong defense. Julia stood at the sidelines and cheered with the rest of the crowd, encouraged by his determination and satisfaction.

The air was raw, mist drifted under the glare of the floodlights, which made Julia wish she could run on the field with the boys, just to keep warm. The blonde who'd driven Nick home was at the edge of the field with two boys, one of whom had his arm around her. Protective maternal juices flowed, smothered by a sudden leap in her pulse. Kate, Maria and Suzanne Branigan materialized at the edge of the crowd, one decidedly attractive male adult in tow.

Julia squinted and ignored her pulse as she tried to determine which twin was in charge of the girls. The man was dressed for the weather in a jacket she hadn't seen either Branigan wear. He grinned and cheered, then said something that made Maria laugh. The mannerisms were indigenous to Drew, endearing in Sean the few times she'd glimpsed them. The giveaway turned out to be Kate. She responded to an adult remark with the bored expression teenagers reserved exclusively for their parents. Julia's heart beat faster.

As the crowd cheered a play, Julia turned back to watch her son. When she looked again at the Branigans, the girls were alone and had taken seats in the bleachers, dishearteningly close to her ex-husband.

"Nick's doing well."

Julia jumped at the deep, familiar voice behind her. "Sean. I didn't know you were here." He looked as though he suspected a fib, but he let it pass.

"Didn't Nick tell you? We talked about it Wednesday."

"No."

"We had quite a heart-to-heart."

"He shares little these days."

"I think he was looking for a male perspective on a few things."

"My parenting skills?"

"Privileged information." He studied her. "This isn't sitting well with you."

"You're right."

They cheered a play. A fine layer of mist clung to his hair and when he looked at her, she could see the minuscule droplets in his eyelashes. "Care to elaborate?"

"Not here, not now."

"Am I allowed to ask how your week's been?"

"It's been all right," she replied.

"Mine, too." He toed the grass. "Look, Julia—"

"It's okay. I didn't expect to hear from you. I didn't want to, remember? I had some thinking to do."

"Good. That's fine. I just wanted you to know that I took your advice. Announced to Kate and Suzanne that they were coming home. There were no handsprings. New house rules, Dad's cooking. We've had a lot of spaghetti. You should come to dinner. Bring Nick next week."

"He did mention that."

"You'd make the perfect buffer."

"The adjustment counselor, come to share some garlic bread? Sean, I don't think so. Conflict of interest."

"Kate's working with her tutor. I thought we agreed that you're no longer involved."

"I'm not."

"Then come as a friend."

"It's not wise. Even this..."

"The soccer game? Drew and Holly usually bring the girls, but I thought it might be fun to scan the bleachers and try to pick out the father of your children and his woman of the moment."

"Woman? Is that what you and Nick talked about?"

"Nick is who we talked about. He's quite a kid, Julia, in all seriousness, a hard worker. You have a lot to be proud of. Kate wanted to see him play. I thought he could use a whole Branigan cheering section." Despite the quip, he seemed uncomfortable, restless. His car keys jangled as he stuffed his hands into his pockets.

"Maybe that's better left to Ryan. He's Nick's league sponsor."

He pulled the keys from his pocket and examined them. "Wrong Branigan in the cheering section?"

"This shouldn't involve him."

His green eyes darkened. "*This?* Do you and I have a *this?*"

"You're teasing."

"Another involvement you'd like to reconsider?"

She looked over her shoulder as though her son might be behind her. "I don't know what I was thinking last Saturday night."

"Frankly, neither of us was thinking. I do, however, know what you were feeling."

"This is no time for humor."

"Did that sound funny? Humor didn't give me insomnia all week."

"A phone call would have been nice. Some indication..."

"You told me not to."

"You're right and I thought I meant it."

"This is the nineties. I'm told you're allowed an occasional phone call yourself."

"I'll call you tonight."

"We can do better than that. The game'll be over by nine and my girls are back up the hill with Drew and Holly. It's their reward for making it through the week at our house."

"It can't have been that tough."

"I'll save that for later. Nick told me he's going into Boston with his father. Forget the phone. I'll drop off the girls and come pick you up. You and I can have a cup of coffee at the Grill, or go into Plymouth if you'd rather. Lots of people, bright lights.''

''No bogs to monitor?''

''No frost warnings.''

''We could both use a little frost.''

Complications arose immediately. The Cottage Grill on the Duxbury Road, the only coffee shop in Mill-brook, was bustling with after-game business and the only free tables were on either side of one occupied by Nick, his father and current girlfriend, who Julia had pointed out at the game. Sean joked about her son's appetite, but her lips had thinned to a determined line and her cheeks were flushed. He suggested his house, then Plymouth.

''I'm sorry. I should have known Nick would be ravenous after the game and they'd stop here on their way to Boston.''

''Are we avoiding your ex-husband or your son?''

''I'd be more comfortable somewhere else.'' Once they were back out in the parking lot, she sighed. ''This is silly. There's no reason why we can't sit in my living room for a while.''

Julia's house was a combination of formality and charm. Not unlike the woman herself, Sean thought as she stood beside him. Her piled hair was still damp from the mist, becoming to her eyes and heart-shaped face. It pulled his attention from the cable-knit cardigan sweater and khaki slacks. She wore clothes well. He couldn't remember seeing her in anything that didn't flatter her face and figure and those wide, dark eyes.

The two of them had left their damp shoes at the front door and there was something ridiculously intimate about standing with her in wool socks. He could feel her watching him now as he glanced at photographs of her sons, a framed watercolor of a barn, fresh logs laid on the fireplace ashes. She went to make coffee and he stared at the hearth, not entirely sure this had been a good idea after all.

Should he wander into the kitchen? Should he wait by the logs? He was no good with women and their expectations, no matter what their age. He knelt and built a fire, which turned temperamental, giving him the excuse to stay in the living room and poke at the kindling. By the time Julia entered, the blaze was as steady as the heat in his chest.

She put the tray on the end table. "A fire. What a nice idea." She asked how he took his coffee. He was tempted to ask for a shot of brandy, but the last things he needed were more heat and fewer inhibitions.

"You're a hard man to figure, Sean Branigan."

"It's been a long week."

"Tell me about the girls."

"I don't know." He sipped. "I don't know if this is about my daughters or your son or about us. Damn it, Julia, you came into my life because of my kids, but if there's something . . . if this goes . . . can you understand that I need to separate this from that?"

"This from that. Yes."

He couldn't read her expression and no elaboration followed. Maybe he'd hurt her, hell, maybe he should back out right now. He stepped away from the flames as his jeans heated. Maybe this wasn't the only fire he was too close to.

"Who's doing the cooking?" she finally asked.

"We alternate." He meant to keep it humorous and focus on Suzanne's inventive stir-fry, his burned cranberry muffins or Kate's rebellion at having to decipher a recipe. One anecdote led to another, however, and with each, Julia listened or suggested or commiserated.

It had been a long time since he'd relaxed in the presence of a woman. His occasional dates were separate from family, any of them. His brothers and their families were built-in buffers between his daughters and his sporadic forays into the world of bachelorhood. In four years there had been no playing house or involving his daughters in short-lived relationships. In four years there'd barely been any short-lived relationships.

There had only been one woman in his life who'd shared his children and fate had forced him to go on without her. His brothers had filled the gap till now, till Julia Hollins had opened doors long shut and forced him to reconsider.

"Sean?"

He blinked. "Enough about my kids. Nick did well tonight, thanks to your insistence that he stay on the team."

"I know you had something to say about it more than once. I guess you got him to think it over. If he used you for a sounding board, that's fine."

"You're hedging."

"No more than you are. I know he'd rather be at the bogs every afternoon. He says the harvest is nearly finished."

They stood at the mantel and watched the flames. "All but the Taft bogs. It's a berry with a later set.

Drew and Holly talked us into buying the acres about five years ago.''

"Somebody told me Holly had originally wanted to sell everything out from under you."

"Holly's a Bancroft. She inherited the house, orchard and Bittersweet Bogs from Peter Bancroft. He worked for my father, then bought Bittersweet and the house from my grandmother. When my parents died, he took on our guardianship so we could stay together. He died about nine years ago."

"Wouldn't it have been logical to leave the boys and house to all of you?"

"He had his reasons, but Holly arrived in Millbrook intending to sell it. Drew changed her mind."

"Branigans can be very persuasive."

"That season was a disaster. We were in debt. Black frost ruined the Bittersweet crop, then Drew goes nose to nose with Holly, who chooses October to show up and claim her inheritance. In the midst of the harvest he got in a fight with Kevin over her. The two of them fell into the conveyor. I was at the firehouse and got the ambulance call. Kevin fractured his leg, Drew broke some ribs. The next thing you know, Holly's here for good, takes over the management of Bittersweet Bogs and she and Drew're living happily ever after. Women, who can figure?"

"Women? One little Holly against six strapping Branigans."

"Exactly my point. Ryan and I even wound up delivering Maria when Holly went into labor in the middle of a blizzard."

"She must have fought that tooth and nail."

"We were all crazy about her by then and the storm was awful. Aren't you tired of Branigan stories?"

"They haven't bored me yet."

"Holly pushed. Ryan and I caught. Piece of cake." He had to clear his throat as his voice caught.

"Sean Branigan, are you choking up on me?"

"Hell no. My brothers and I've been through a lot together, that's all."

"I hope you were there for Kate and Suzanne's arrival."

Sean turned from the flames to find Julia's gaze wide and kind, as he knew it would be. He leaned back and closed his eyes. "Annie was a trooper. From a man's perspective it's a damned miracle, every time. Then they make you take the little miracles home without a warranty or instructions." The shock was how easily this reverie had come, how good it felt to share it. "I'm sorry. I didn't mean to ask you for coffee with the intention of dwelling on this. I'd rather talk about Nick."

Julia seemed to glow from the color thrown by the flames. He lifted his mug and absorbed her smile, as rich and dark as the coffee.

"Nicholas arrived forty-five minutes after I went into labor. I pushed. Paul caught. Piece of cake. Unfortunately he didn't come with a set of instructions, either."

"Neither do marriages."

"A diplomatic way to ask about mine?"

"Maybe."

"Too young. Too poor, then too rich . . . Paul's got some wonderful qualities, but he wasn't meant for monogamy. No regrets, though."

"Brett and Nick?"

"Yup. Nick's proud of what you've taught him. He says Jody explained the complicated process of buying some acres no longer in production. It involved the Clean Water Act, the Wetlands requirements, EPA standards."

"That was the Taft property, now part of Bittersweet Bogs."

"It must help to have an environmental attorney in the family."

"Jody would be the first to tell you that we pushed him in that direction. He gets his hands dirty, though, just like the rest of us. If the berries ripen by the end of the week, I'll finish up with Nick out there."

It was Julia's turn to study the flames. "I thought Ryan would be in charge of Nick when he worked. He mentions you far more often these days."

"Does it matter?"

Julia's answer was a long time coming. She put her mug on the mantel and turned to face the room. "I'm beginning to feel as you do."

"So we're back to that again. I admit a lot of us weren't Millbrook's best role models, but those days are long gone. Unless you count Kate's smoking in the locker room."

Julia smiled, but she took the poker and adjusted the logs. "It's no different with me, Sean. I worry about who's involved in my children's lives. The boys do a decent job of separating their father from his— entanglements. I worry about the message it sends."

"And yours? Message? Entanglements?"

"It's ironic that both of us were involved with each other's children." She squatted as she reached into the ashes.

Sean looked down at the thick, dark crown of her hair as firelight flickered over it. The floodlights from the barn had given it the same highlights. It was fastened with tortoiseshell combs and he imagined it loose, as it had been that night a week ago. That night.

"I can't seem to separate what has to do with me," she murmured.

"I don't understand." He did, though. He saw her clench her jaw and close her eyes. Her breasts were rising and falling in a rhythm that matched his own rapid breathing. *She feels it, too. She knows as well as I...* He put his hand on her hair and when she cocked her head, he pulled the combs, one at a time, and placed them on the mantel.

She left the poker on the hearth and stood. "I don't know if I can separate this from the rest of my life the way you do."

He was already touching her hair, sliding it off her shoulder. *This.* He had no idea what *this* was beyond a sweeping sense of calm, sliced down the middle by exhilaration. "But you'd like to give it a shot?"

She grinned and patted her cheeks. "I keep telling myself this heat, this flush comes from the fireplace, but I'm tempted to make an inappropriate analogy between you and those blazing logs in there."

He put one hand over hers. Again she closed her eyes and this time raised her face. His exhilaration became physical. *This* took definition. The pads of his fingers tingled over the soft swell of wool. He circled a single pearl button when he kissed her, small kisses that teased and tormented. She tasted of her coffee and smelled of her same shampoo, all things Julia, all things new and enticing, things already familiar.

She kissed him, thigh to thigh, warm as the fire. Pleasure engulfed him and it wasn't until Julia tightened her fingers over his wrist that he realized he'd worked open half her buttons. He laid back the sweater, just off her shoulders. Her bra was a half-cup sort of design that cradled her breasts and left most of the skin exposed. She glistened in the firelight.

"Magnificent."

"So you've said."

He smiled, but she put her hands back over his as he cupped her breasts.

Her eyes were dark, smoldering, but there was caution there, too, and wide-open trust. He kissed her again and pressed his forehead against hers. After three deep breaths he whispered, "You have an empty house tonight."

"Our behavior's been careless enough."

"We need a smoke alarm." He laughed, then lost himself in her eyes. Brown, flecks of gold from the fire, passion and pleasure and reason: everything that was this woman seeped into him and tempered the hard edge of arousal with something closer to contentment. He leaned forward.

Over her sweater he kissed her breasts, then hugged her. The embrace was a neat, perfect fit, made snug by her arms across his back and her head in the crook of his shoulder. They breathed together. She nuzzled against his chest, her cheek over his heart. He closed his eyes and played with her hair. This was how it might feel if she were in his arms in his bed. Hollowness yawned; the hole ached to be filled.

Slowly she put her hand over his and traced his wedding band. He was sure she felt him tense. He held her tighter, against the scrutiny of those wide, deep eyes.

"After all the reminiscing about childbirth, you must think of Anne at moments like this."

"Not in ways you might think. It took a year. I spent the next one making peace with my loss and the one after that making peace with myself."

"And that peace comes from disconnecting part of yourself, your physical self, from the rest of your life?" When he didn't answer, she pressed his chin. "It's a fair question to a man in a wedding band who's unbuttoned my sweater."

"The rest of my life contains two very vulnerable little girls who've been disrupted enough without being exposed to a string of women in and out of their lives."

"Have there been a string of women?"

"No." Sean leaned back against the wall. "There've been times when it's been important to feel—something—anything."

"Just to see if the plumbing still works? To feel connected? Sex can do that."

He winced. "I'm a cranberry grower, not a psychologist."

"You're also an emergency medical technician, someone who already knows how to disconnect, as you put it, who can pull away emotionally."

"Someone who has to. You make me very much aware that I'm a man, Julia, but yes, I guess I pull away." He brushed back his hair. "I'm sorry if you were expecting me to say something else."

"Don't apologize. You're protective of what you love. Your loss is nothing like mine and I'd be the last one to judge you. Sometimes we behave out of instinct. Sometimes we just hang on to whatever gets us through the day. Or the night."

"You would have gotten me through tonight very nicely."

"And there we'd be at breakfast, all grim and apologetic or stupidly bright and nonchalant. No thank you."

Coffee and conversation were finished. He poked the fire one last time as she took his arm. "I think I'd better walk you to the door."

"Julia, I have no intention of hurting you."

"Neither of us is a stranger to pain, Sean."

Eleven

When the door was shut and the Jeep gone, Julia went back to the fireplace. She bent and poked the embers as deeply as she'd poked at Sean. She'd had no right to pry or maybe she had every right. Everything from Sean Branigan's demeanor to the tone in his voice had confirmed it. Surely he knew it was her own preservation instinct.

When a knock at the door was followed by a rush of cold air, she spun, expecting him, relieved that he'd realized she'd spoken out of self-preservation.

"Hey, Mom."

"Brett!"

"I probably should have called first. I drove down with some friends to the swim meet tonight against Wheaton. I thought I'd swing by and see if that navy parka of mine is here. It's getting cold in Cambridge and I need it at school."

Julia recovered from her shock and crossed the room. "It's in your bedroom closet. Take the gloves and hat, too."

"You okay?" he asked as he hugged her.

She touched her hair. "Yes. Just surprised to see you. I was drying my hair in front of the fire."

"The other guys are out in the car. I thought it might be okay if we stay over. I'm supposed to meet Dad and Nick tomorrow afternoon so we'll drive back to Boston in the morning."

She studied her eighteen-year-old. "Why stay over? Have any of you been drinking?"

He shook his head. "I swear. The meet ran late, that's all."

There were four of them, all freshmen, new friends enamored of what turned out to be the women's division of the Harvard University swim team. Julia invited them in, then went up to strip Nick's bed. The rest was up to the boys and she laid out sheet sets and towels on all four single beds in her sons' rooms.

When she returned to the living room for the coffee mugs and her hair combs, Brett and his friends were going through a loaf of bread, the remains of her deli meats, a six-pack of soda and a bag of pretzels in front of the fire. It felt like old times.

In exchange for a very late breakfast before the trip back to Cambridge, Julia's houseguests hauled leaves she'd been raking into the backyard compost pile. The night's fog had begun to burn off and the day was crisp and clearing. She slipped Brett twenty-five dollars and her last box of cookies with her final hug as a now-familiar Jeep pulled up at the curb.

In response to her son's raised eyebrows, she explained that Nick's boss had dropped by after they'd run into each other at the soccer game.

"Mr. Branigan wouldn't have anything to do with *two* empty mugs on the mantel last night, would he?" Before she could manufacture an answer, he laughed. "You hot ticket."

"Brett Hollins, I am not a hot ticket."

"Maybe Mr. Branigan thinks so."

She jerked her thumb north. "Since you brought it up, I made it very clear to him that I am not in the hot-ticket category. Harvard Square is waiting."

"So's the cranberry grower."

When she finally reached the Jeep, Sean had lowered the window. "Guests?"

"Brett and some college friends."

"I was just passing by."

"This is a dead-end street."

"I've been at the station doing some EMT paperwork. I thought we should talk—about last night."

"Which part of last night?"

"Damn it, Julia, I'm up all night feeling lousy about the way we left things, pacing around the bogs, driving my brothers crazy while I work up the nerve to come over here and you're—pleasant."

"I can be hostile, if you'd prefer."

"You tie me in knots. I'm not good at this. I haven't had any practice."

"Which part have you come back to practice?"

"Getting you out of your sweaters."

"That, dear heart, you manage quite nicely. I'm just sorry you left so disappointed. Did you really expect me to invite you upstairs for a little—connecting?"

"It was worth asking. I didn't know what to expect. That's why I'm here. We need a real date, the kind where I pick you up and take you out, someplace besides your office, my bogs or your living room. Of course I wouldn't mind if we wound up back there."

"At my office."

"Preferably your living room, fire and all, but first lunch."

"Is this a bribe?"

"Could be."

"Then I decline. Brett and his friends arrived not five minutes after you left last night. The front door wasn't even locked. Can you imagine if they'd arrived ten minutes earlier?"

"Or fifteen minutes later if we'd followed our instincts."

"Instinct has me chewing my nails. I need time to figure out what the heck's going on with us. Sooner or later you're going to have questions, too, and I'm not at all sure I have any more answers than you do. I know so much about you—and so little. I don't know what you're used to, or looking for. We aren't Ryan and Sky, two hormone-enraged teenagers out on the bogs, or even Drew and Holly battling it out in neighboring houses on your compound. I'm a very public figure who answers to the school administration, not to mention the parents of Millbrook. My behavior has to be above reproach."

"No Jeep parked in your driveway at all hours?"

"This is smack in the middle of town, dead end or not."

"I was kidding. I have my own concerns, you know. One's fourteen and one's twelve."

"Even if I were nothing more than a country neighbor, I'm still the only decent role model my sons have."

"Decent role models are allowed to leave the house. Come with me now. You pick the spot. Brett's left, Nick's with your ex-husband, and Megan, God bless her, parked her own kids with Bridget so she could spend a 'girls' day' in Boston with mine."

"I'd rather you didn't mention this to your brothers."

"That must mean yes."

"I think it's a good idea, believe it or not. How about Duxbury? It's a healthy drive from Millbrook. There's an inn with a restaurant in the village, and a view and a beach. Or we could have some lobster salad at the waterfront."

"Lobster salad would be a good distraction." His voice softened. "Julia, since I lost Anne all the women I thought I'd ever need for help have been my in-laws."

"For emotional support?"

"I know you want to offer the same thing. I should never have headed in the other direction with you, but I don't know that this is any better."

Even alone at the curb she whispered. "Sean, I'm not sure either one us knows where we're headed."

In the three weeks since they'd met, the foliage had begun to turn in earnest. The countryside from Millbrook to Duxbury blazed with everything from maple trees to hedges. The inn was a converted sea captain's house in the heart of the historic district which ran along Snug Harbor. Lunch was still being served in the barnlike addition and the atmosphere was as good as the lobster. Julia talked about her family, a sister in Annapolis and her parents in suburban Baltimore. They compared summer stories: her boys' escapades on the Chesapeake since the divorce, his girls' love of their New Hampshire camp since the loss of their mother.

They walked the historic street, smiled at home-owners raking leaves and kids coming home from soccer and football games. They noticed the similarities of the imposing shipbuilders' houses to Ryan and Sky's and joked about inland Millbrook at the turn of the nineteenth century trying to keep up with the prosperity of coastal towns linked to the China trade.

"Quintessential New England, imposing, yet understated," Julia said.

"You and the architecture." Something inside him began to open again, to tug and rearrange the parts he'd been so good at keeping separate. He kissed her in front of a Chippendale fence. She kissed him back.

"You give a woman pause, Branigan," she managed as she caught her breath.

Contentment taunted him and he slung his arm around her, tight. His happiness, her presence intensified memories he had never anticipated. It had been four long years since he'd felt what Julia revived in him. These emotions had been put to rest, emotions he doubted he could sustain again. This wasn't a night in a woman's bedroom, a stolen weekend at a remote inn.

The wind was brisk off the water, but they stayed at the harbor long enough to watch lobstermen and musselmen bring in their catch. Julia pointed to the strip of barrier dunes across the tidal basin. "Let's drive out to the beach."

It was a natural request, one he should have anticipated. "Just as pretty here."

"Come on. We'll get some shells, a few mementos.
I love it this time of year, brisk, deserted.... We can
walk off lunch, then get back to Millbrook and real-
ity. Come on, you old cranberry grower, you got me
this far." She wove her arm through his and grew serious. "Sean, don't shut me out. You got me this far,
I'll get you the rest of the way."

He watched the flag snap on its pole at the harbor
master's office and filled his lungs with the pungency
of low tide. Julia tugged and they retraced their footsteps to the inn and his Jeep. On the short ride out she
commented brightly on the houses, landscaping, a
view of the harbor that reminded her of Maryland's
Eastern Shore, and the spit of dunes and beach that
kept the Atlantic at bay. The banter continued to the
parking lot. Her efforts were Herculean.

They parked and walked over a dune, edged in snow
fencing to preserve the fragile grasses, and paused at
the top as the view opened. Out at the water line a
couple jogged with a collie between them. A single
lobster boat headed for home.

The tide was ebbing and they left hard-packed
footprints as they walked, kicking aside occasional
driftwood or the shell of a horseshoe crab. She seemed
content without his conversation and they settled instead into the rhythm of the sea's rumble, the gulls'
swoop and caw.

He'd known it was a mistake before they'd crossed
the dune. His chest felt laced with rawhide. There were
coals in his throat.

"Have you spent much time here?"

"Yes."

Julia gathered sea glass and polished stones in a bag she'd found in the back of the Jeep. "I like any beach best at this time of year. Everybody's gone back to their real lives, back to obligations."

He nodded. They walked. When they'd reached the half-mile mark in the snow fencing, they turned to retrace their steps. Before starting back, however, Julia opened his hand and dropped half a dozen of her treasures into it. He moved them around with his index finger.

She picked up an opaque piece of sea glass from his palm. "This was clear as a windowpane once. How long do you suppose this glass has been tossed around out here to get so worn down? A year, four years?"

"Long time." He knew the minute he raised his eyes he'd find that deep, coffee-colored scrutiny.

"Maybe this glass was glittery and bright for eighteen years, Sean, then it was shattered. Maybe four years of tossing and grinding against the sand has made it this opaque."

She held it between her thumb and forefinger and ran her other hand behind it. "It's beautiful in its own way, but it's not what it was. No glitter, very little light gets through. Just shadow." She dropped the sea glass back into his palm and her glance never wavered. "I'm not as insensitive as I appear. The old Sean Branigan seems to have surfaced about the time I suggested the beach."

He stuffed the glass and stones into his pocket and she snuggled into his shoulder. "It's not hard to imagine that Anne was a big part of this."

The sea breeze whipped loose tendrils of Julia's hair across her face and blew his in half a dozen directions. The surf rolled and pounded the way his heart repeated its incessant thumping. He nodded finally and kissed her hard.

Julia put her hands on either side of his face. "She wasn't part of my living room, or even that inn we just left, not even the bogs in a romantic way, but this opened the wound." She bent again to the stones. "I'm so sorry."

He knelt in the sand. "I'm the one who should apologize." As sure as the tide would turn and come back to fill their footsteps, something was returning in him, filling the hollow place, something he still pushed aside out of self-preservation.

Twelve

He put his arm around her. "This isn't for you to work out, it's for me."

"Then I think it's time to go back to Millbrook."

"Yes, I suppose it is."

They made conversation in an atmosphere that wasn't strained as much as it was melancholy. Sean had expected to scale a mountain and had simply reached a plateau—level ground, to be sure, but no heights had been reached.

When they finally arrived at Penham Road, Julia sat for a moment as the Jeep idled in her driveway. "I press. I'm sorry."

"That's your expertise. You expect a lot from us, that's all. Maybe too much."

"I apologize for the beach. Maybe for my house last night, too. I'm pragmatic and meddlesome sometimes. I shouldn't bring up Anne every time we're in a clinch."

"A clinch?" He smiled.

"My life is good, Sean, sweet, settled. It's what I've made it and I'm satisfied. More than satisfied."

"Julia, you don't have to tell me all this."

"Quiet. I memorized it all the way home and if you start to interrupt or argue, I'll chicken out. I own my house, manage the mortgage, get along with my neighbors. I take pride in my career. I like to think I make a difference in the lives of the children I work with."

"Not just children."

"Thank you. I have my life all mapped out and five years ago I was anything but a cartographer. It took determination and effort. I'm very pragmatic."

"So you've said."

"So you can see why I react as I do, why I keep bringing up Anne at the most inopportune moments. I can't seem to let go of analysis, of having to understand, to know the reason for everything."

"I'm not sure I have reasons to give you." He waited. "Or maybe there are so many I can't separate the ones that are important."

"They're all important."

"Yes, I guess they are."

She pulled his hands to her mouth and kissed his palms, then brought them to her breasts. "I wanted this, too, when the time was right. You talked, I talked last night. There's no denying the chemistry between us. Things were lovely, more than lovely, but we should have stopped there for a while. I'm asking for more than you can give. I see that. It took the beach, so I'm glad it happened now rather than later. It's not

your fault. This afternoon proved that I've misjudged everything. Our timing's off. We're rushing
toward disaster, Sean. I couldn't stand another one
and you sure don't need it, either."

His throat burned, blister raw and with his jaw
jammed shut, he hugged her, hard enough so that she
was all flesh and bone and warmth against him. He
kissed her mouth and her cheeks, surprised at the
tears. He wiped them and pushed at her hair and
brushed sand from her temple.

"Anne was part of everything that was part of me,
Julia. When I lost her, I pushed this part of my life
aside out of self-preservation. I've given you everything that's left in me. I thought it would be enough.
You're right. I don't know why that should surprise
me. You've been right about every other aspect of my
life. It's too soon. I shouldn't have gone back to the
beach."

"With me or ever?"

He winced. "I should have gone back alone first."

"In many ways you are alone, Sean. Still."

Julia met the Boston bus at the Plymouth terminal
Sunday evening. As usual, Nick was pensive and tired
on the ride home.

"Homework finished?"

"I can take care of my assignments."

"Did you hook up with Brett?"

"Yeah."

"Where'd you go?" she asked in an effort to draw
him out and clear her head of her own reverie.

"Different places." He looked at her sideways. "We
hung around on Newbury Street some. Danielle took

us to some gallery. She knew Brett's art professor and he was having a show or something."

"How nice." They lapsed into silence again as she took the highway exit and turned out toward the sand hills.

"I saw Mrs. Branigan with Kate and her sister. Some hair place by the gallery."

"Did you? Newbury Street's a popular spot." She glanced at the now-familiar landmarks as she entered the Millbrook town limits. "Brett was here Friday night—did he tell you? I gather he's got his eye on somebody on the swim team. There was a meet at Wheaton."

"Elsa Langsford. He tells me a lot, Mom."

"Brothers should, Nick. I hope you'll always have each other to confide in, now that the battling years are over."

"Whatever." He scrunched in his seat and studied the new compact discs in his lap. Yes, his father had bought them for him. No, they hadn't agreed on another weekend visit. Business would keep him busy till the holidays and he had made plans to be in Palm Springs for the Thanksgiving.

"With Danielle?"

"Well, not with Brett and me."

"I'm sorry. But your grandparents would love for us to go to Baltimore for the holiday. What do you say?"

"I'm working at the bogs weekends and the guys say there's a lot going on over Thanksgiving, some parties and stuff. I'd rather just stay here."

"I thought your job would only go through the harvest."

"Ryan has work for us." He looked at her sideways, then out to the passing landscape.

Preoccupied—both of us—she thought. From Plymouth to Millbrook Nick's sporadic conversation was interspersed with her reverie of Sean on the beach.

Well after dinner, after the dishes were done and she sat in bed with an unread book open in her lap, she still thought about him. Those eyes, the warmth of his hands on her breasts, *her* warmth in his arms...what if she had made love to him? How could a man who made her feel so connected be so disconnected himself?

For that one she had no answer. She had her own life and children to consider, neither of which she was willing to jeopardize for a brief affair with a pensive, introspective, tight-lipped widower. The hell of it was Sean Branigan had understood. He'd sat there in her driveway and held her and agreed.

Brooding men, fighting personal demons as the sea licked their heels, was the stuff of literature and film. Only in fiction did the story end with the embrace and the wind and the optimism. Even those story lines fast-forwarded six months or a year rarely held up to her analytical eye. Whoever said wisdom came with age was probably the neophyte who thought up the saying love was lovelier the second time around.

At five-thirty Monday evening Kate came bounding into the kitchen fresh from a shower. It looked to Sean as though she had mascara on her lashes and blusher on her cheeks but he held his tongue. "So, Dad, I need a ride to Dr. Hollins's."

His stomach muscles tightened. "May I ask why? You just got home from soccer. Dinner—"

"I have to interview somebody for an English assignment, you know, go to their house and take notes about what they do and stuff. I sort of forgot to mention it. She's so worried about my work, and all, I thought she would be a good choice."

"You've already asked her?"

"Yes, in school today."

"Any reason why you can't buzz down to her office and do this during school?"

"She has a job, Dad. Besides, the kids might think I got in trouble again or something if I went to her office." She opened the refrigerator and said to the milk shelf, "So, is Nick Hollins going to work for us for a while longer?"

"A few more weekends, then as needed. Why?"

"No reason. Dr. Hollins said Nick would bring me home."

"That's not for Dr. Hollins to decide. He's a teenage driver."

"What's with you? He has a perfect driving record."

"Not so perfect."

"Come on, you're his boss. You let him drive our trucks, even the eggbeater. Do you think he'd do anything dumb with me in the car? If you come back and pick me up, I'll feel like a total child. You're not going to wreck this, are you?"

"The English assignment or the drive with Nick?"

"I'll totally die if you say something to him, like 'Remind Kate to wear her seat belt.'"

Sean raised an eyebrow, read his daughter's true intentions with the ease of a suspicious father and followed her to the car. He also followed her to the front door on Penham Road.

In contrast to his fleece pullover and faded jeans, Julia looked fresh, appealing, and as striking as ever, but subdued. She was back to her professional and personal reserve. As usual, her eyes were wide and inquisitive and the only hint that she might be working at the effect was the flush on her cheeks, more natural than his daughter's.

"Hello, Sean. I told Kate that Nick can drive her home, or I will, if you'd rather."

Kate shot daggers at him as Julia showed her into the living room. He looked across at the mantel and couch and back. "Nick will be fine. Thanks for doing this. I didn't know anything about it."

Kate grinned.

"No reason why you should. This is Kate's assignment. There's lasagna baking. She can have some supper with us when we finish."

"All right. Don't make it too late. She has other homework." Green eyes scrutinized brown. Brown eyes scrutinized green. "How's your week going?"

"It's only Monday. Anything can happen."

He cocked his head, but she didn't elaborate.

"We're out at the Taft bogs finally."

"Later berries."

"Yes. I'll see Nick this weekend."

"Fine." He reached for the door, then turned back. She looked beautiful, composed, yet there was something in her expression he couldn't read. "You all right?"

"Are you?"

"Question with a question," he replied, wishing Kate weren't within earshot.

"Hard habit to break."

He searched her face and ached to hold her. "Julia?"

"Kate's waiting," she said gently. "This is important."

Sean nodded and went home to instant rice and hamburgers with Suzanne.

Thirteen

___

Tuesday Sean left Suzanne setting the table and Kate muttering over her math assignment as he hustled to the family vegetable garden for some end-of-the-season carrots. Although the brothers had scattered for dinner, Nick was getting out of Julia's car in front of the barn.

The teenager was still in his soccer shorts and team jacket and he paused as Sean called him. "Looking for somebody? I think we've all gone for the day."

"Ryan said I could use your pump."

"Game today?"

"Practice."

"We're coming Friday night."

"Suit yourself." He started for the door to the barn.

Sean decided to pass comment on the teenager's sarcasm. "Care to spill your guts?"

"What's that supposed to mean?"

He waited till the boy turned. "Something's eating you. I'd like to help, if I could. When I get moods like this from Kate, I walk around on eggshells trying to figure out what's eating her. Never worked worth a darn with her and it's a flat-out failure with you. So I'm asking outright if I can help."

"You can't, all right? Not the way things are."

Sean put up his hands. "Thought it might be Kelly. Girl trouble. I'll back off. But I'm here if you change your mind."

The boy leaned back against his car and crossed his arms over his chest. His scrutiny of Sean seemed endless before he finally spoke. "Look, I know about you and my mother, okay? Brett figured things out when he dropped in. He put the pieces together."

Sean paused. "So that's it. Your mom's a wonderful person."

Nick's glance, piercing and direct as Julia's, never left him.

"Nick, she's helped me a great deal with Kate. This isn't easy for me. She understands that. She's a very loving person. You have nothing to worry about."

"Keep the kids stupid."

"I wouldn't have said that, but there's no reason to involve anyone else right now. I hope you can understand."

"I understand plenty." He opened the trunk and pulled a bicycle tire out, then headed for the barn.

"Good," Sean replied. "Nick?"

The boy turned at the barn door.

"Is this privileged information, too?"

"Mr. Branigan, I think you've screwed things up enough with my mother without telling her I know all about it, too." He went into the barn and closed the door.

The encounter replayed itself endlessly. To discuss it with Julia would betray a trust, and Nick obviously felt betrayed enough. Sean thought about his own children. He thought about Julia. Most of all he thought about himself and the murky waters in which he was struggling. He was up to his hips in a bog and it wasn't cranberries he was trying to corral.

"Look, Dad, just chill about it, okay? I'm fine. Everything's fine. You don't need to worry about every little thing in my life."

That night Sean stood at Suzanne's bedside and offered her an extra quilt. "I'm here if you need me, how's that?"

"Fine."

He said good-night and pulled her door closed, as confused as when he'd first gone in to say good-night.

"So, Dad."

"So, Kate." Sean stood at his usual spot at the bedroom door that night, relieved by the decidedly cheerful tone emanating from the mound of pillows propping up his eldest daughter. His retriever whined at his heels.

"Puck wants to go out."

He ruffled the dog's fur and nodded. "See you in the morning. You're in better spirits than your sister. I just tried to say good-night and she's still talking through gritted teeth."

"You didn't try one of your heart-to-hearts with her? She broke up with Brad so chill for a while."

"Broke up? She's too young to date. Who's Brad?"

"The guy who calls her at Uncle Drew's. It's a phone thing. Hanging out at school, you know. Didn't you notice that Brad Morino was with Tiffany Millis at the soccer game Friday night? Dad, the whole sixth grade's talking. Tiffany had the nerve to sit next to Suzy at lunch today and talk about him."

He sighed at Kate's you-are-hopeless voice. "Is there anything I can do?"

"Not unless you're a sixth grade boy." She scrutinized him with one of her pensive expressions. "You mad at me?"

"Never."

"Yeah, right."

"Not right now, not today, how's that? Why, sweetheart? What made you think I might be?"

"Something's been bugging you. Forget it."

"Bugging me?"

"You're all kind of, I don't know, shadowy. Not there. Like not knowing about Brad and Suzy—you know, stuff."

"I'm sorry. I've had a lot on my mind this week, stuff that has nothing to do with you, so don't worry. I'm fine. You're fine, too."

"Then could we talk about me for a minute?" When he nodded, she closed the magazine propped on her knees. "You know how you want us to stay here all the time now, and be a family and all that? Then could we please do something about this room? I don't want to hurt your feelings." She lifted the comforter. "But lamb sheets and teddy-bear wallpaper. Even the triplets think it's babyish." Kate's bottom lip suddenly trembled.

Sean crossed the room and sat on the edge of her mattress. "Katie?" She waved him away, but he leaned forward. "Why haven't you said something before?"

"You and Mom designed it for me." She blinked at the bears. "I didn't mind so much when I was staying up the hill and everything. Aunt Holly let me decorate the guest room. But here...even my friends tease me."

"Sweetheart, this isn't a shrine to your mom. She'd change it in a minute if she were here. I guess I didn't notice how—babyish it is."

"This whole house is a shrine." Kate closed her eyes and leaned back, then sat up and smiled. "It's really all right? I mean to change at least this part? Aunt Megan told me you might say yes. I bought some posters with her."

"Posters?"

"Save the whales, Woodstock, awesome ones of James Dean and Jimi Hendrix. You'll love them. They're totally retro."

He sighed. "Teddy bears to Woodstock. The fifties, sixties and seventies . . . totally retro."

She leaned for Puck and rubbed his ears. "You're not such a bad father, you know."

"Thanks, sweetheart. What brought that on?"

"Aunt Megan sort of talked to Suzy and me in Boston. She says you're kind of going through this mid-life crisis thing and feeling all guilty about being a crummy part-time father. She says I've been giving you a tough time. I guess I just want you to know that I understand about the part-time stuff. I don't mind so much."

"I wasn't aware that you minded at all."

She shrugged again. "I'm lucky. I like this arrangement. It's just that sometimes it feels like I'm—I don't know—in the way at the other houses. Everybody's busy with their own stuff and little kids. They take a ton of work, you know."

"I remember."

"Do you? Weren't you always at the fire station or sleeping off your night shifts?"

"Is that how it feels?"

Another shrug. "When I think about being little, I mostly remember Mom."

"I hope you do think about your childhood, whether you remember that I was there or not. I was, Kate. I always will be. I'm sorry Mom can't be."

As she nodded, he groped for words and pushed back the lump that threatened to choke them before they were spoken. "Katie, for a long time I've thought we had the perfect solution to losing Mom. Five aunts who love Suzanne and you...who could ask for more?"

"It's okay, Dad."

"I hadn't thought about—imposing on Erin and Holly or Sky or the others."

"I knew I shouldn't have said anything."

"Of course you should have, maybe sooner than this, darling. Dr. Hollins isn't so sure, either." He waited and searched her face for the infinite nuances that made her so readable. He expected the usual bark or denial, or affirmation that her life was perfect.

"No really, it's fine. In the beginning being with my aunts and uncles helped me not miss Mom so much. It was good for me, really. Things are better now. Suzy and I are in the way, sometimes, that's all. They'd never tell you." Tears rose over her lashes.

"Kate?"

She held him off with a gesture. "I'm okay. Really. Everything's fine about Mom. I have her in my heart and all that."

"Then what is it?"

"It's just sometimes I wish I had another mother. Please don't be mad at me for thinking that. Sometimes—" She drew her knees up. "Never mind."

"Talk to me, Kate. I'm not angry, not at all. You won't hurt my feelings. I'm listening, I promise. No shadows."

"It's just that you look and act so much like Uncle Drew. Sometimes I wish Aunt Holly had a twin, too, for you, somebody we wouldn't have to share with cousins. I know that's dumb but everybody's busy with their own kids, with the triplets or Mack, or Hayley and Sophie. Even in Boston Aunt Megan was great, but she worried the whole time about her own kids—if Aunt Bridget remembered Evan's ear medicine, if Flynn would take his nap away from home."

Sean leaned and hugged her, magazine and all. "Why on earth haven't you said anything?"

"Because I know there could only be Mom for you. You never date or anything. You're never sad about being by yourself." She sniffed and laughed. "Of course you never are by yourself with all the Branigans around here. I know all my aunts make everything okay for you just like they try for me."

He nodded against her temple, against her fancy Newbury Street haircut and her child's perception. "Sweetheart, maybe it's time that you and Suzy stop being brave for me and I stop being brave for you."

"Dad?"

"We need to step into the light. Then maybe we can start to fix some of the things that have been broken for too long."

Kate leaned back into her propped pillows. "That's how it feels, I guess, like something's broken. Something needs to be fixed. It's been a lot of years."

"I know." He kissed her forehead and stood as Puck whimpered again to go out. "Thank you for making me see it. I love you, Kathleen Ryan Branigan."

"I love you, too."

He closed Kate's door as she snapped off the lamp.

His bogs were quiet and cool, though well above freezing. His bogs. His brothers. Puck sniffed at the sand pile and Sean moved through the shadows. Shadows had swallowed him whole for days at a time in the beginning, shaped and shaded his life until escape had become habit. Shadows had soothed them all.

Sean walked. He circled the pond, the pump house and the deep gray stretch of dike to the cart path. He walked and jammed his hands into his jacket pockets, surprised at the feel of forgotten treasures. At the courtyard in front of the barn, the bright beam of rafter-hung light sliced the darkness. Sean stepped from the shadows and opened his hand.

The polished sea glass glimmered dully in his palm. He played it in his fingers, ran his thumb along the worn edges. He raised his face to the October night. Pine tops whistled softly. He inhaled the aroma of his brother's wood stove. Puck found him and the two of them stepped back into the shadows toward home. He dropped the stone back into his pocket.

Slowly then, but without hesitation, he worked his wedding band over his knuckle. With a soft *clink* it joined the stones and glass in his pocket. As he retraced his steps along the dike, he rolled them all through his fingers, then pressed his fist against the plane of muscle below his heart, against his gut.

Fourteen

———

By the time Julia turned her car onto the lane marked Bittersweet Bogs on Wednesday, her heart was in her throat. She passed Drew and Holly's farmhouse and wound down the hill to the courtyard that separated Kevin's house from the barn, which served as headquarters for the family operation. Trucks, cars and four-wheel-drive vehicles, all of which she recognized, were nosed up against the picket fence that delineated the vegetable garden. Puck was sniffing happily among the pumpkins.

Kevin arched a single eyebrow as he appeared in the first open bay of the barn. "Not much to watch today, I'm afraid."

"I thought I might find Sean here."

"He went to the house to get some paperwork. Kate all right?"

"Yes. I just thought I'd save him a trip to school. I need to tie up some loose ends and I was out on my lunch hour."

"Go on over." He pointed across the pond. "Take all the time you need. Tell him I said not to rush."

"Thanks."

She waved off the brothers with a pounding pulse and sweaty palms that she wiped on her trench coat as she knocked at the front door. Sean answered with a flush already squarely in place across his nose. "This is a surprise."

"Your brothers said you were here. I lied through my teeth and made up a conference about Kate."

"You're here about something else?"

"Probably not appropriate. Spur-of-the-moment decision."

"Spur-of-the-moment. Encouraging."

She let him take her coat and he put down a sheaf of papers as he laid it over the banister. He was dressed in jeans and a chamois shirt close to the color of his eyes. His gaze never left her.

"My pragmatic, mapped-out life has been shredded. I know you have things to work out. Pressure from me won't—"

He put his right hand against her mouth and held up his left. Her chin quivered and her throat burned. "Oh," came out as a husky whisper as she ran her thumb along his naked ring finger.

"It's time, Julia. I'm raw with it, turned inside out."

She nodded.

"If you hadn't come to me today, I'd have come to you. You're what I want in my life, all the corners of it. Staying disconnected has taken so damn much work and energy I finally realized how hard I've been fighting the one thing that might make me happy. I want to love what you love, *who* you love. I want you to love us."

She nodded and leaned back against the door. "Me, too." The moment her shoulder blades touched the door, he pulled her forward into a bone-crushing, life-affirming hug. She snuggled, rearranged herself to fit the length of him, already tight, anxious. She felt the thunder of his heart.

"Can you stay?" he whispered.

"For a little bit."

"I have to get back to work, too."

She smiled up at him. "Kevin said not to rush."

"Kevin hasn't spent the month of October fighting this aching, lusting, craving desire for you."

When she spoke again, they were at the top of the stairs, in his bedroom doorway. "Are you sure?"

"I went to the pharmacy the morning we went to the beach. Emotionally I've been in a black hole, but physically I've been sure since you dangled under that scarf in your office."

"I never *dangled*."

"Julia, darling, no one dangles better than you."

She glanced into his bedroom with her heart in her throat. "And here?"

"Yes, here."

She worked open the buttons of his shirt as he unzipped the back of her dress. It slid neatly off the ends of her fingers, down her hips. Her bra was another lace-covered design, peach, modest satin, catching the light.

She took his hands again, and kissed his palms. "Then this is where you get to expose the magnificent breasts."

Making love to Sean Branigan was like nothing she had imagined. After all the soul-searching and anguish, she'd expected hesitancy or regret. Instead, he was aggressive and amusing and out of his clothes before he reached the bed. Her combination of modesty and desire seemed to be all the aphrodisiac his body could stand.

She sat next to him on the edge of the mattress. Her bra had a tiny clasp between the cups, which opened as he pinched it. He slid the lace to either side and palmed the softness until she panted and arched. He combined desire, admiration and pleasure into a slow, steamy smile that became a wet erotic trail over every inch of her exposed flesh. She gasped softly and played with his hair, held his head as his eyelashes brushed her overheated skin. "You do make up for lost time," she managed.

"This is for the bogs," he whispered as he kissed her breasts. "And this is for the orchard. The soccer game, your living room..." With every caress she sank deeper into a haze of sensation.

"The beach," he finally murmured in her ear as she returned the strokes. "The beach and this endless week, which forced me to see what I was so close to losing."

Julia sank into the sheets and pulled him with her, shifted under him and nuzzled against his face. This first time had to be perfect. She was determined to give him pure physical and emotional release, an act that would cleanse the soul and confirm a future. This time was to be Sean's. She kissed him hard and deep and when the rhythm of his body matched hers, she ran her hands shoulders to hips along the length of him.

Pleasure already transformed his features. He hovered above her, looked at her with that smile and those eyes and then came to her.

She cupped his hips playfully, pushed him deeper, and rose to match his rhythm. He whispered her name. Pleasure intensified, teased her with gooseflesh, then sudden bone-deep heat.

"Sean!"

He balanced on his elbows. Now with each thrust he ran his tongue over her breasts, one then the other. She arched. A thunderbolt of ecstasy ripped through her. She pulled him back down, clung to his neck, welcomed him as he quickened his rhythm and followed her into deep, life-affirming release.

They lay still for long, tranquil moments. In the hall a clock ticked softly.

"Julia." He played with her hair. "You make me feel like one of my brothers. As if it's a very long time ago and my whole life's in front of me. You make me feel connected again, to everything I packed away."

"To life, Sean."

"It's been a long time," he finally whispered.

"Me, too."

Sean slid his arms under his head and watched Julia as she stood at the mirror in front of Anne's empty dresser. She finished buttoning her dress and repinning her hair and came back to the edge of the bed. He closed his eyes and smiled as he felt her run her finger along his lip.

"There's a bunch of cranberry growers waiting."

"Mmm."

"You all right?"

He opened his eyes. "Never better."

She glanced around the room. "This wasn't as easy as I thought—being here, in Anne's place. I didn't think it was what you wanted."

Sean sat up and pulled her into his arms again. "Katie talked to me last night, really talked. She feels the loss in ways I never imagined. She wants a mother, Julia, her own, unshared, in-her-own-house mother."

"She's never talked about it before?"

"From what I can understand, she was afraid to rock the boat. She thought I was happy with the arrangement, with things as they were. The hell of it is, I thought I was. I thought we all were." He kissed her. "I didn't think this could happen twice in a lifetime. There was no point in searching for what I never thought I'd find. Now that I have, I realize what a commitment I'd be asking you to make—taking on all of us."

"No more than what would fall into your lap. Nick might not be as easy as the girls."

"We've already had words."

"You didn't tell me."

"I ran into him yesterday at the barn. You and I weren't as close as we are now." He grinned. "Even so, I got the feeling it was a man-to-man discussion, so I kept it between us. He's protective of you."

"I have been rather...out of sorts this week."

"Kate accused me of being shadowy. It's the child who got the adult to think."

"They run on purer emotion and logic. We could all take lessons."

"I'll leave Nick to you for the time being, then," Sean replied.

She handed him his shirt. "Thank you. For all the reasons I've already given you—school, my position, your enormous family, the children—promise me we'll keep this between us for a while longer, till we're sure."

"I'm in Providence all weekend for a regional EMT meeting. Nick can work. I won't be around to stir up anybody."

"What a pity," she murmured.

"You can keep a normal schedule."

"What's normal?" She smiled. "I hope your daughter told you what a good job she did interviewing me."

"I got the usual one-word answer from her when I asked. She seems to have a thing for Nick."

Julia kissed him. "Nick's got the same feelings for one Kelly Baxter. I think she comes with a built-in set of car keys. Treat Kate's heart as carefully as you've treated your own. Her crush will fade. Some eighth grader will sweep her off her feet."

"I'd just as soon not have anyone sweeping her off her feet just yet, thank you. One Branigan in the throes of love is enough."

When they finally returned to the foyer, Julia put on her coat and suggested he wait in the house while she walked back to her car.

"I hate this, already," he muttered into her hair. "Stolen moments on lunch hours. Trumped-up excuses to call you will be next. What's left, a quick fling out on a bog?"

She ran her finger along the shell of his ear and whispered, "It worked for your brothers."

Fifteen

Sean found a dozen reasons to call Julia and more than that for why he couldn't. She was working; she was away from her office. One or another of his brothers might wander into the barn behind him. Kate needed the phone; Suzanne had a call. Kate and Suzanne were listening. He dreaded being gone over the weekend.

He worked side by side with Kevin, Drew and Ryan, and pushed himself to exhaustion in his battle against raging hormones. One or another of them mentioned her name with maddening frequency. He snapped, swore and flushed into his scalp when he realized they mistook his moods for trouble with Kate.

He didn't deny it; it was the smoke screen he was after, but he grew more pensive as they tried to drag information out of him.

Monday she surprised him again in front of his brothers at the barn. The moment the two of them entered his house, he nearly made love to her standing up in the foyer, pressed back against the front door. That afternoon he stood with her at Kate's soccer game, barely able to concentrate on the action in front of him.

Halloween fell on Tuesday and Kate, all sincerity and benevolence, volunteered, then insisted on chaperoning her three-year-old cousin Hayley on her first trick-or-treat outing. Only as far as Penham Road, she assured Sky and Ryan, who were delighted to stay home with the baby and greet the hordes who wandered down Main Street.

Sean's twin took Suzanne with his children, which left Sean equally delighted to drive his eldest daughter into the village and walk with her, much to Kate's disgust.

Julia opened her door in a witch's hat and black leotard, flattering enough to jump-start his adrenaline system. She insisted they come in for cocoa and sat them at her kitchen table. Nick appeared briefly, mentioned a compact disc Kelly had loaned him, and after a glare from his mother asked Kate if she'd like to hear it.

As Hayley sipped from her mug, Sean put his hand over Julia's and squeezed it involuntarily as she ran her bare foot up under the cuff of his chinos, hidden from view by the tablecloth.

Friday night he took the girls to the high school boys' soccer game and feigned surprise at meeting Julia. Nick played half the game and managed to make two outstanding saves. Sean followed Kate's glare to a striking blonde cheering the soccer player wildly from the sidelines.

"Nick's fan club giving you some competition?" he tried.

"Dad! There's nothing going on with Nick, okay?"

"Okay."

"He's practically in love with Kelly Baxter. It's all he talked about on Halloween. Boys are such jerks. All they care about are girls who drive fancy cars."

"Some. I'm going to sit with his mother. Want to join us?"

"No way."

Frost warnings were called but with only the Taft bogs with fruit, he put in his shift between the end of the game and his daughters' bedtime. Julia Hollins beside him would have warmed him nicely.

The surprise was Saturday. Daylight saving time was over and the weekend seemed to shrink along with the light. The brothers were twenty-four hours into the harvest of the Taft bogs and final "trash flooding" of the rest to skim the harvested acreage of hulls and debris.

They worked under full sun and brisk wind. Despite Sean's compliments on his game and attempts at conversation, Nick wasn't much warmer than the bogs. It was a side he saw more often in his child than Julia's.

Close to lunch, as Ryan gave instructions to Nick and other seasonal workers, Drew took Sean aside. "Any plans for tonight?"

Sean shook his head. "Muscle rub and a good night's sleep, why?"

"Ryan's over there offering the League boys dinner and a movie when they finish. I'd like to do the same with your girls." His green eyes flashed. "I thought you might need some more time with the adjustment counselor."

"Kate's doing fine."

"I'd like to see her old man do the same."

"Look, Drew, whatever you're thinking—"

"Give it up, twin. I'm not asking for any details. We just thought we'd open your calendar a little, beyond an occasional lunch hour."

"We?" He glanced at the rest of them.

"All right, Holly came up with this. I mentioned the conspicuous absence of your wedding band. She's got it into her head that there might be more to you and Julia than concern over Kate's behavior, and if so, you might be trying to keep the kids out of it for now."

"Not to mention my brothers and their overactive imaginations. What am I, dinner conversation?"

"It's been awhile since there were any bachelor Branigans to speculate about."

Both men were needed at the conveyor and the discussion died, but not before Sean agreed to Drew's suggestion.

"I hear Ryan's springing for pizza tonight," Sean commented.

"I guess so," Nick replied.

Sean stripped off his waders and offered Nick a hand. Though Nick merely shook his head, Sean continued. "You guys deserve it. Good game last night, by the way."

"Thanks."

"Season's almost over."

"I know the schedule."

"Right."

"I don't think it's us," Julia said later over pasta with mussels. "Nick's been moody since his weekend in Boston. I think maybe it's Paul and the change of plans for Thanksgiving, or this on-again, off-again thing with Kelly. He swears he doesn't care, but he's been a bear all week."

"Have you talked to him about us?"

"No. He's hardly in the mood." She covered Sean's hand with hers. "What would we discuss without the trials and tribulations of our children?"

"Our own, no doubt."

Julia had picked the spot, an out-of-the-way waterfront restaurant in Plymouth with a small dance floor and seafood menu. Her view included floodlighted beach, moored fishing boats and the decidedly handsome cranberry grower who'd surprised her with the invitation.

"We should talk about us. This euphoria will wear off, Sean, and you'll be stuck with the same pragmatic, meddlesome psychologist you met that morning at school."

"And you'll have to contend with a weather-beaten, dog-tired farmer fire fighter."

"Yes, I know. How'd I get so lucky?"

"Can this work? Twenty years ago I would have been far too rough, too provincial for you. You would have been too intellectual, probably too focused and too analytical for me."

"But it's not twenty years ago. I love a man on the rebound from eighteen years of wedded bliss. That's what's terrifying."

"Who better to show you the ropes? I want that stability and happiness again. I want it for me and I want it for the girls. Julia, damn it, I want it for Nick and Brett, too."

Tears clung to her lashes, which pooled then blurred her vision. "My one shot at this was far less successful."

"Then you can make up for lost time."

"Time. How much of it do we give this? When do we stop the analysis, the tiptoeing around your family and the kids?" She reached for his hand again. "I'm scared to death, but even now, I can't imagine giving you up."

"Then marry me. Now, before you change your mind. Save all the adjusting and analyzing for afterward."

"This from a man who couldn't stand on the beach with me?"

"The last fragments of another life."

"I'd like to think that afternoon was a bridge to our future."

"It was, thanks to you and my talk with Kate. It wasn't so much a change of heart after that, but more like I found it, if you want the truth, found where the hell I'd packed it away."

"Cold storage. Packed away for safekeeping until the time was right. Anne would want that, Sean. I feel sure someone who made you so happy would want to make sure that wasn't lost. Any mother would want that for her children, but I know she'd want it for you, too. She'd want her family whole again. Oh, darling, of course I'll marry you."

Sean's reply was a long time coming. "I think," he said finally, "at this moment I love you as much as I've ever loved anyone in my life."

She leaned to his ear. "And if you'll take me home and get me out of this dress, I'll let you prove it."

Julia leaned against the Jeep's headrest and savored the anticipation and desire that made the full blush of love so irresistible. Sean's four-wheel-drive vehicle hummed as they headed for Penham Road. She opened her eyes as he slowed down. The unlighted road was deserted.

"The Taft bogs?"

"Mmm."

She looked at the hulking shapes of the parked harvesting equipment as he pulled onto the property. He drove over the path toward the wooded boundary and stopped in a secluded corner.

"Something need checking?"

He turned from the steering wheel. "Julia, darling, you and I have never done a foolish, reckless thing in our lives, except fall in love with each other. Just this once let's not be pragmatic."

"Here? It's November. I have a perfectly good, warm, comfortable bed, an empty house..." Desire had teased her since they'd left the restaurant and the vision of Sean, all shadow and moonlight in the seat next to her, intensified it a hundredfold. She began to laugh. "No frost warnings? No brothers likely to show up?"

He turned off the ignition. "Nope and there's a fat harvest moon just hanging up there, too good to waste on a bedroom."

"I have to admit the car is all heated up and I'm not far behind." She smiled, savored the thunder in her chest and the transformation of the man she loved as he slid out of the Jeep. "Good heavens, Sean, I thought you at least meant inside."

He came around and opened her door. "And waste that moon and these bogs? I dare you, Dr. Hollins. Make love to me out here. Let me give you something I've never shared with anyone else."

Despite the game, under the bright brittle moonlight his expression told her more clearly than words how important that was. The beach had sent him backward and this would propel them forward, together.

"I dare you," he repeated.

Before she had time to change her mind, she opened her sweater, the blouse underneath and then the tiny plastic clasp. When her breasts were fully exposed, she knelt in the pine needles. "I dare you back, Branigan."

She gave herself up to sensation as she aroused him. The heat of his mouth on her cold skin, the rough ground and soft mat of pine needles under her coat, the warm flat planes of his body that responded so wonderfully to her touch created passion that engulfed her. This was risky and uncomfortable and sexy and wild.

"You're right," she gasped as she clung to him. "Never—I've never."

"When you marry me," Sean gasped, "all this will be yours."

She groaned and laughed and kissed him in every spot she could reach. Sean was everywhere at once as she rose to meet him, heavy then weightless, playful, then serious. The cold night vanished as he stretched over her, his hard body all the blanket her overheated skin needed. They locked out the world until they were oblivious to anything but what they were to each other.

"Thanksgiving's in two weeks. I want you and the boys to spend it with us. It'll give Nick something to focus on besides what he's not doing with his father. It's the perfect time to ease the kids into this and tell them we plan to marry. It will also be the true test of your Branigan stamina."

Julia sat snuggled under Sean's arm in front of her fireplace. She pulled a pine needle from his sweater. "I can hardly imagine all of you in one house."

"We use the homestead—Kevin's. It's a nostalgia thing."

"I shudder to think what it was like before all those brothers got married, a veritable testosterone festival."

"Endless televised football games with a little turkey on the side. Not a bad day."

"And now?"

"Sky tried to civilize us once. Herbed turkey, gourmet side dishes, linen, silver, crystal, china. We had to sneak into her library to turn on the football games. Since then we've compromised. We're back at Kevin's. Everyone's casual, there's too many children not to be. Some touch football outside if the weather's decent, buffet dinner when the kids get hungry. These years there's always a new baby or two napping upstairs."

"Sounds wonderful."

"It's a good place for you and the boys to start. Controlled chaos and all that. Nick and Brett will be the oldest by far, nice for Kate, though."

"Nick and I haven't discussed anything yet, mostly because I thought he'd work out the moodiness by himself. He likes all of you. He's been so happy working at the bogs it doesn't make sense."

"I can try another heart-to-heart with him, as Kate calls them. He'll be back first thing in the morning."

"If it comes up naturally, that would be fine. Otherwise, I think it's time I talked to him. Sunday dinner, as soon as he gets back."

"And Brett?"

She kissed his shoulder. "The night he surprised me and found the two mugs and my hair combs on the mantel he called me a hot ticket."

"You are."

"I believe his advice was, 'Go for it.'"

"What wisdom."

Sunday, since Jody her husband was at the bogs, Megan arrived with paint chips, wallpaper books and her boys in tow to help Kate plan the transformation of her bedroom. Sean left them to their designs.

As he crossed the dike to his brothers, he thought about the larger transformation that lay ahead for all of them. Nothing would be as simple as a new coat of paint or a more sophisticated wallpaper, but if anyone could work magic as a stepmother it was Julia Hollins. It was Nick who gave him pause and his own ability to touch that place the sixteen-year-old was guarding so fiercely.

Mentally he'd approached the boy's frustration from every angle. The solution still eluded him, partly because he was still mystified by the problem.

As he reached the vegetable garden, Nick and Matt Branigan emerged from Ryan's four-wheel-drive vehicle. "I'm trying to convince your hired hand that a career in medicine is less strenuous than nursing ailing cranberry bogs," Matt said.

"You get about the same amount of sleep," Sean replied.

The teenager's response to the banter was a steady, noncommittal glance in Sean's direction.

The weather had turned. Wind whipped off the wide, flat acreage and cut through jackets and waders. Tempers flared. Megan and Kate delivered a pot of chowder and deli sandwiches; Erin crossed the courtyard with a thermos of coffee and sodas. The brothers grumbled about everything and worked with numb fingers as they pushed to finish the season's manual labor.

By four o'clock the group had reassembled at the barn to store their waders and clean equipment. Matt's wife and toddler had arrived for dinner with Kevin's family. Holly called from the hill to suggest that she and Drew spring for Chinese food. The mood lightened.

I can have this again, Sean thought as he watched them. *I've found someone who can put things right.* His sister-in-law had been correct to call it a *heart thing,* but he had been right, too. Love, the kind that was going to blend and sustain, was a *gut thing,* too. Few things in the past troubled years had felt as right as this. Sean's contentment was sweet.

He approached Nick on the cobblestone courtyard as he pulled the elastic suspenders from his shoulders. "Pretty rotten weather. Always finicky this time of year."

"Whatever."

Sean took a steadying breath. "Nick, your mood's obvious. A week ago you gave me some idea of what was bothering you. I think maybe we'd better talk, whether you want to or not. Your mom's as worried about you as I am."

"I'm not the one she should worry about."

Sean caught Ryan's glance but waved him away. "Let's take a walk."

"Right. Can't make this too public. If you're going to tell me it's just one of those things that happen between adults you can save your breath."

"It is and it needs to be discussed." He peeled off the waders and slung them over the fence.

"You're such a hypocrite."

"Nick—"

Whatever reserve the teenager held snapped as Sean reached for him. Nick slapped his arm away and spun on his boots. He lunged and caught Sean full force in the mouth and chest with his shoulder.

The two of them fell backward into the pumpkin vines and spent zucchini, splintering the picket fence as they went. There were no punches, but the force of the blow took most of the wind from Sean. He swore again as he grappled, nearly outpowered by the strapping soccer player. The two of them struggled and rolled from pumpkins to the brussel sprout stalks.

"What the hell is this?" Ryan yelled as he ran to them.

Matthew yanked Nick off his brother and fell with him into the potato hills. "I didn't come out here to make a house call on my day off. Settle this without fists."

As if Matt were invisible, Nick flailed again at Sean. "She's in love with you," he cried through gritted teeth. "You with your stupid lectures and your friendship. You lying snake."

"Nick!" This time Sean hauled him to his feet himself. "Listen to me."

"No more advice." The boy's voice broke as he threw off Sean's grasp. "No more! You can cheat on your wife all you want, just choose somebody else to do it with and don't ask me to keep quiet about it. Find somebody who won't give a damn what the soccer team and my friends think. Somebody who won't have to pretend nothing's going on when she sees your kids at school. Don't you think about that stuff? Stay away from me, while you're at it and keep Kate away. I can hardly look her in the eye."

Sean put his arm out but Nick flinched and drew a fist. He hesitated, then pressed it against his swelling cheek. He swore into his sleeve and swiped at his eyes.

"Married? Who's he married to?" Ryan finally repeated as Kevin pulled him up out of the dirt.

Through a gloss of tears, Nick glared at the Branigans. "He asked me to keep it quiet two weeks ago. He's hitting on my mother. You're his brothers. If you knew why didn't you do something?"

"Married!" Sean spit debris and blood as he strong-armed him. "That's what this is about?" Relief drained what energy he had left. He began to laugh, then tried not to as the boy's expression darkened. "I'm not married."

"Right. Let me guess. You and Mrs. Branigan got a divorce this afternoon, right after she and Kate brought the chowder over."

"Megan made the chowder. That Mrs. Branigan?" Jody said.

"Who the hell else?"

"Nick, I'm married to Megan."

"Then I've got her name wrong. The one in Boston with Kate." He jammed the air with his finger. "The one across the pond *at your house,*" he added as he glared at Sean.

The two of them stood spent and panting. Bits of zucchini fell off Sean's sleeve. Nick pulled brussel sprouts out of his hair.

"You've got the person right but the relationship wrong. My wife died four years ago, Nick. Megan is my sister-in-law, and yes, I love your mother very much." Sean put his arm around him. "Can you walk?"

"Course I can walk."

"Will you listen?" Sean added through gritted teeth as his youngest brother inspected his lip.

"Make him listen in your kitchen. You both need ice packs," Matt said.

As Nick pressed his cheek, Sean turned to the small, fraternal crowd that had gathered on the cobblestones. "Finish up for me," he said to all of them. "I've got a lot of explaining to do."

"To more than Nick," Ryan called.

"What does he mean he's in love? When the heck did that happen?" Matt picked rotted pumpkin from his waders.

"While none of us was looking," Ryan answered.

Sean motioned to Nick. "Except this guy. For now, this is between us." He picked his way through the splintered fence and waited for the teenager to follow.

Julia arrived at the saltbox colonial with a change of clothes for her son and a pie she'd made that afternoon. Suzy and Kate had set the table and looked as anxious and confused as she felt. Sean was standing in front of the family room fireplace holding ice to his lip as the flames crackled. His hair was damp and his clothes were fresh. Nick stood next to him, flushed, equally damp, wrapped in Sean's oversize terry-cloth robe. He, too, had ice pressed against his cheek.

"Somebody had better start explaining," she said as she crossed the room. "Ice packs? Sean, you never said anything about injures. I thought Nick fell in. Was there an accident out there?"

"You're not kidding," Kate replied.

"Misunderstanding. Chivalry is alive and well in the Hollins household," Sean muttered from behind the crushed ice and dish towel.

Julia looked from one to the other. "You've been fighting! Sean—"

"I started it," Nick mumbled.

"Whoa. You slugged Dad?" Suzanne asked.

"I didn't slug him, okay?"

"They got in a fight over you, Dr. Hollins," Kate said. "And nobody'll tell me anything."

Nick glared at his mother. "If you'd told me what was going on, this never would have happened. Who else was I supposed to think Mrs. Branigan was? She was here making dinner. She was in Boston. She and Kate brought lunch this afternoon. She's got red hair," he muttered as a final explanation.

"You think Dad likes Aunt Megan? Nick, if you weren't so moon-faced over Kelly Baxter, you might have some idea of how stupid that is," Kate replied.

Nick glared. "And if you weren't hanging around me all the time, you wouldn't even know who Kelly Baxter is. Give it up, Kate. You've got everything about your father backward. You're even more clueless than I was."

Kate's green eyes darkened as she blushed. "About what? You're not even making sense."

"We're the ones they wanted to keep stupid."

"About Aunt Megan?"

"Wake up. About your father and my mother."

Julia stood rooted to the hearth as the color drained from Kate's complexion. She looked at her father and then up at Nick. "But your mother's Dr. Hollins."

"And your father's my boss."

Confusion swept contempt from Kate's features. Her shoulders slumped and she blushed furiously again. Julia's heart ached, but as she stepped forward, Sean held her back.

Kate thrust the clothes at Nick. "Put your junk on. You look really stupid in my father's robe."

"You better get used to it. You'll be seeing a lot of me in bathrobes once we're all one big happy family." He took the bundle and headed for the powder room.

"What big happy family?" Suzanne mumbled.

Kate turned for the door, but this time her father stopped her. "While Julia and I decided how we felt about each other, we tried to keep all of you out of this." He leaned to Julia. "Your son thought I was married to Megan."

"Married! That's the reason for all his moodiness? Why didn't he say something?"

Sean smiled ruefully. "He did just now."

"That really makes me feel great. My own father having secrets with Nick Hollins," Kate added.

Sean put his arm out to his daughter, who ignored it. "Nick was as confused as you are. The only way to straighten this out is to put everyone on the couch. We have some talking to do. Yes, Julia and I want to be married. We want all of us to be a family."

"What on earth ever made me think we could put this off till Thanksgiving?" Julia whispered.

"Married?" Suzanne repeated.

"A family. Here, in this house?" Kate asked.

"How many bathrooms have you got?" Nick added as he came back in jeans and a sweatshirt.

"Not enough. Daddy, how could you?"

"Kate, you and I talked about it."

"About another mother, not about boys moving in. Not about *this* boy living here." Kate called the dog. "Puck wants to go out."

"He's asleep," Nick replied.

"Then I want to go out, okay?"

"The rule book says you two don't have to act like siblings until after we're married," Sean threw in despite the fact that everyone glared at him.

The storm door slammed as Kate marched into the dusk with Puck at her heels. Sean shook his head. "She's a Branigan. Let her go walk off the steam. She'll be back."

Julia nudged her son. "Nick, go after her. It's the least you can do for Sean after nearly knocking his teeth in."

The teenager blushed. "Jeez, Mom. I feel stupid enough already."

"Suzanne, you, too."

They both grumbled but they both went.

"As usual I completely misjudged my daughter."

"This has more to do with Nick moving into Kate's space than my becoming her stepmother. She had to give him up to Kelly Baxter, now she has to share a bathroom with him. Let them adjust to the idea—" They both looked up at the sound of a muffled roar. Sean frowned. Fear stopped Julia's heart as her "What on earth?" was interrupted by a distant scream.

Recognition suddenly distorted Sean's features. "Oh my God, the sand." Sean was on his feet and out the door without another word.

In his twenty-year career as a fire fighter and emergency medical technician, Sean Branigan had answered three calls involving sand piles. Two had been to the gravel company at the edge of town, the other to bogs like his own. In the dusky light he raced over his lawn to the dike and blocked the mental image of the crushed victims he hadn't been able to save.

Suzanne was running to him from the opposite direction. Behind her, at the far end of the bogs where the hill rose, a raw alcove of exposed tree roots lay where the mounded sand had slid away.

"The sand fell on him," Suzanne cried between sobs as her father reached her. "She tried to stop him and then the sand began to slide."

"Nick?" Julia arrived breathless beside him.

"Puck went digging after something. He was growling and crazy to get it and the sand hill started to slide. Kate ran into it and started to dig him out and Nick said not to. He yelled at her but the sand just slid and slid all over."

Suzanne turned and ran with them. The entire left side of the hill had flattened across the cart path. A pine sapling lay bent in half from the weight with another hanging at a sickening angle. From the back side of the mound, the retriever limped into view.

"They're over here." On the far side of the slope, Kevin Branigan had run from the barn, shovel in hand, to the ridge. He called instructions over his shoulder to his wife. Matt slid down between the pines and jumped clear of the sand.

Stay professional. Sean gripped Suzanne by the shoulders. "Go up to Aunt Erin's and stay there."

"This won't be like it was with Mommy, will it?"

Truth. He was already leaving her. "I don't know yet. Aunt Erin's, Suzy. Now."

He reached the sand just behind Julia, who plowed through the shifted drifts at the periphery of the mound. On the far side of the hill, tucked nearly out of view, Nick Hollins was trapped on his knees, buried to his waist with Kate.

"Don't move them," Matt said as they loosened the sand.

Kate's head and shoulders and one jean-clad leg were exposed. Nick had wrapped his right arm around her and pressed her face forward into his sweatshirt against the threat of inhaling the granules.

"Mr. Branigan." Nick's voice was a broken whisper.

"Hush, son. We'll get you out." Sean knelt behind Nick and attempted to support him by his shoulders as Kevin dug around him.

The teenager muffled a scream. "It hurts," he said through gritted teeth.

Kate managed to whisper, "I'm sorry," as Julia and Matt freed her and laid her gently backward, taking the pressure off Nick's chest. Julia knelt with her and brushed back her hair as they waited.

Sean soothed his frustration at not being able to hold his daughter by sinking into a tirade on risk and safety and knowing better, broken by the distant wail of Sean's ambulance and crew and a single piercing groan from Nick as he tried to raise his left arm and reach for Kevin.

"You don't have to write so small."

Kate finished her signature on Nick's cast with a peace sign and flower. "I'm leaving room for Kelly. She'll want to put hearts and kisses all over your arm when she finds out what a hero you were."

"Give it a rest, kid."

"She'll probably have to drive you everywhere in that dumb car."

His medicated grin was slow. "I hadn't thought about that."

"Yeah, well, I'm sorry about your dislocated shoulder and your broken arm. I guess this wrecks soccer."

"I wanted to quit awhile back, anyway."

Kate tried to swipe at her eyes, but the tears kept coming and her voice broke. She looked at Nick and sank gingerly into the sofa cushions as she put her hands over her face. "I know it was all my fault. I nearly killed you."

Nick adjusted his sling. "You cracked a bunch of ribs so I guess we're even." He pulled her hands down.

"Come on. I never know what to do when girls cry. I'm not mad or anything. If anybody should be ripped it's your dad. You should see what I did to the pumpkin patch. There was zucchini all over your uncles. They yelled at me to stop and I didn't even listen."

Kate smiled. "I'm not so good at taking orders."

"Get used to it. Brett's bossed me around all my life. Now I finally get a little sister to take up the slack."

"Will you ever drive me places?"

"After this mess, I'm probably grounded for life. I did kind of slug your dad."

"I sure hope your mom's a better cook than he is. Nick, you know Andy Collins, the goalie? Do you think you might ever invite him over?"

"I thought I—" He paused and closed his eyes. "Sure, maybe."

"It'll be nice not being the oldest cousin anymore. Now it'll be you and all the baby-sitting."

"How many are there?"

"Ten, not counting Kate and me," Suzanne answered.

"Ten's not so bad, it looked like fifty little kids that day at the bogs."

Sean and Julia listened to the family room discussion from the kitchen as they made a pot of coffee.

Sean ground the beans. "How'd we raise such self-centered kids? I don't think any of them give a fig that we're bursting into their lives. All they seem to care about are their own relationships."

Julia poured in the water. "Nick's respected you from the beginning, loved you, too, probably. That's why he was so devastated when he thought you were cheating on your wife.''

"Never have. Never will." He kissed her longer than was wise and opened the floodgates of emotion. "Kate told me in the emergency room that she's fantasized about you as a stepmother since Nick first mentioned that his parents were divorced." He pulled her against him. "Life is so damn fragile. I've wasted enough of it. I want a second chance with you now. Julia, make us a family."

"I will, darling."

"I want you in my arms, in my bed, there at dinner, there in the morning. That can't happen until we're married. Thanksgiving weekend, injured kids, limping dog and all the Branigans.''

"I have family, too."

"We'll squeeze them all in, every last one," Sean said.

She kissed him hard and held him against her. "I can't think of anything Brett and Nick and I need more."

Epilogue

Since his first daughter had married into the family, it was Hugh O'Connor who proposed the Thanksgiving toast every year. As senior member of the extended family, he began with a prayer for those who were no longer with them. When tears were wiped he continued with a raised glass and toast to what he called "the celebrations of life." The following year was no exception.

Hugh inhaled deeply. "I don't know what smells better, the turkey cooking in this brand-new kitchen or the fresh paint and new lumber."

"Depends on how hungry you are," Sean called with his arm around Julia.

"To Sean and Julia's first anniversary."

"Second Thanksgiving—" Julia added.

"Third house, if you count the two we sold to build this—"

"And four children," Sean said.

"Who needed this union as much as their parents," Drew added.

While Branigans scattered to begin touch football outside, to set tables and baste birds, Sean stayed with his wife at the family room window. Above them their bedroom shared the view and, by design, their children had separate suites on either side, bathrooms and privacy for all.

Their view was southerly, of Bittersweet orchard and the slope that fell away to Kevin's homestead, separated from them by stands of birch and sugar maples. The bogs were just visible off to the right, harvested and put to bed for another season. Across the pond the saltbox colonial from another life now sheltered Jody and Megan and their boys.

On the lawn beyond the French doors, Brett and Nick separated and set up the teams of cousins and parents, balancing them by size and age as fairly as possible.

"Positively bucolic," Sean said. "Nobody's on duty at the hospital or the police station or the firehouse this year."

"Nobody's going into labor, in a cast or propped on the sofa."

"The day's not over yet."

"No matter what it brings, I'll love you. Now and forever, Sean Branigan." She pulled a lump of tissue paper from her pocket. "Happy first anniversary."

Sean pulled apart the layers. In the middle lay a single piece of clear glass shard.

"You're the one who's let the light in," he whispered as he dropped the shard into the porcelain dish of beach stones, shells and sea glass on the table next to them. "Now and forever."

* * * * *

Get Ready to be Swept Away by
Silhouette's Spring Collection

Abduction
& Seduction

These passion-filled stories explore both the dangerous
desires of men and the seductive powers of women.
Written by three of our most celebrated authors, they are
sure to capture your hearts.

Diana Palmer
Brings us a spin-off of her Long, Tall Texans series

Joan Johnston
Crafts a beguiling Western romance

Rebecca Brandewyne
New York Times bestselling author
makes a smashing contemporary debut

Available in March at your favorite retail outlet.

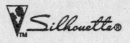

Take 4 bestselling love stories FREE

Plus get a FREE surprise gift!

MONTANA
Mavericks

Stories that capture living and loving beneath the Big Sky, where legends live on...and mystery lingers.

This January, the intrigue continues with

OUTLAW LOVERS
by Pat Warren

He was a wanted man. She was the beckoning angel who offered him a hideout. Now their budding passion has put them both in danger. And he'd do anything to protect her.

Don't miss a minute of the loving as the passion continues with:

WAY OF THE WOLF
by Rebecca Daniels (February)

THE LAW IS NO LADY
by Helen R. Myers (March)

FATHER FOUND
by Laurie Paige (April)
and many more!

Only from ▼ *Silhouette*® where passion lives.

 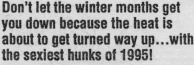

Robert...Luke...Noah
Three proud, strong brothers who live—and
love—by

THE CODE OF THE WEST

Meet the Tanner man, starting with
Silhouette Desire's *Man of the Month* for
February, Robert Tanner, in Anne McAllister's

COWBOYS DON'T CRY

Robert Tanner never let any woman get close
to him—especially not Maggie MacLeod. But
the tempting new owner of his ranch was
determined to get past the well-built defenses
around his heart....

And be sure to watch for brothers Luke and Noah,
in their own stories, COWBOYS DON'T QUIT
and COWBOYS DON'T STAY, throughout 1995!

Only from

SILHOUETTE... Where Passion Lives

Don't miss these Silhouette favorites by some of our most
distinguished authors! And now you can receive a discount by
ordering two or more titles!

SD#05786	QUICKSAND by Jennifer Greene	$2.89	☐
SD#05795	DEREK by Leslie Guccione	$2.99	☐
SD#05818	NOT JUST ANOTHER PERFECT WIFE		
	by Robin Elliott	$2.99	☐
IM#07505	HELL ON WHEELS by Naomi Horton	$3.50	☐
IM#07514	FIRE ON THE MOUNTAIN		
	by Marion Smith Collins	$3.50	☐
IM#07559	KEEPER by Patricia Gardner Evans	$3.50	☐
SSE#09879	LOVING AND GIVING by Gina Ferris	$3.50	☐
SSE#09892	BABY IN THE MIDDLE	$3.50 u.s.	☐
	by Marie Ferrarella	$3.99 CAN.	☐
SSE#09902	SEDUCED BY INNOCENCE	$3.50 u.s.	☐
	by Lucy Gordon	$3.99 CAN.	☐
SR#08952	INSTANT FATHER by Lucy Gordon	$2.75	☐
SR#08984	AUNT CONNIE'S WEDDING		
	by Marie Ferrarella	$2.75	☐
SR#08990	JILTED by Joleen Daniels	$2.75	☐

(limited quantities available on certain titles)

AMOUNT	$	
DEDUCT: 10% DISCOUNT FOR 2+ BOOKS	$	
POSTAGE & HANDLING	$	
($1.00 for one book, 50¢ for each additional)		
APPLICABLE TAXES*	$	
TOTAL PAYABLE	$	
(check or money order—please do not send cash)		

To order, complete this form and send it, along with a check or money order
for the total above, payable to Silhouette Books, to: **In the U.S.:** 3010 Walden
Avenue, P.O. Box 9077, Buffalo, NY 14269-9077; **in Canada:** P.O. Box 636,
Fort Erie, Ontario, L2A 5X3.

Name:_____

Address:_____ City:_____

State/Prov.:_____ Zip/Postal Code:_____

*New York residents remit applicable sales taxes.
 Canadian residents remit applicable GST and provincial taxes.   SBACK-DF

V Silhouette®
TM